Finley Flowers

2 BOOKS IN ONE!

BY JESSICA YOUNG

ILLUSTRATED BY JESSICA SECHERET

PICTURE WINDOW BOOKS
a capstone imprint

Finley Flowers is published by Picture Window Books
A Capstone Imprint
1710 Roe Crest Drive
North Mankato, MN 56003
www.mycapstone.com

Text © 2016 Jessica Young

Illustrations © 2016 Picture Window Books

Library of Congress Cataloging-in-Publication Data is
available on the Library of Congress website.

ISBN: 978-1-4795-98502 (hardcover)

Summary: Finley is thrilled when her teacher announces
the third grade Invention Convention — after all, she has
tons of Fin-tastic creations sure to impress the judges.
And when an upcoming field trip to the local art museum
requires her to answer the question "what is art?" Finley is
ready to tackle the assignment with her usual flair!

Editor: Alison Deering
Designer: Kay Fraser and Kristi Carlson

Vector Credits: Shutterstock ©

Printed and bound in China.
007912

TABLE OF CONTENTS

For Wesley and Clara, who love
thinking up brand-new things

TABLE OF CONTENTS

Chapter 1

A NICE DEVICE

"I love fourth grade!" Finley Flowers announced to her best friend, Henry Lin, as they walked to their brand-new cubbies in the fourth-grade hall. "This year we're the oldest ones here, the head honchos, the reigning royalty of Glendale Elementary School! Remember what Ms. Bird said? We're role models for all the younger kids."

"That's a lot of pressure," said Henry. "I hope we don't disappoint her."

"We won't," Finley told him as she hung up her jacket. "We're going to dazzle and amaze her. This is going to be our year!"

Finley and Henry were just starting their second week of school. So far it had been Fin-tastic! Their new teacher, Ms. Bird, had caramel-colored eyes that lit up when someone asked a question, and her hands fluttered around when she talked. She said "interesting" a lot, and Finley could tell she really meant it. It seemed like Ms. Bird was interested in everything, including all of Finley's Fin-teresting ideas.

Finley was trying extra hard not to be too hoppity in class — they were still in their getting-to-know-you phase. But sometimes it seemed like Ms. Bird was hoppity, too, flitting up and down the rows of desks as everyone worked.

So far their class had conducted "What-Floats-Your-Boat?" experiments, designing model ships to see which ones were the most buoyant. They'd also built bridges out of pretzels and eaten them at snack time. Finley couldn't wait to see what they'd do next.

When Finley got to her classroom, the first thing she noticed was the giant plastic lightbulb and strands of twinkling lights that hung from the ceiling. At the back of the room, she saw a bulletin board that read "Inventor Center." It was covered with pictures of all kinds of crazy contraptions. A robot dog was scurrying around the classroom, fake-barking and wagging its tail. It stopped next to Finley and Henry, and its eyes lit up with heart symbols. Then it fake-whined and lifted its leg.

"Aaaah — no!" Henry yelped, jumping back. "Do I look like a fire hydrant?"

Finley laughed. "Who brought that to school?"

"Ms. Bird did," Olivia Snotham said from behind her. "Its name is Tesla, after the guy who invented robotics."

"Wow," said Finley. "That's some class pet."

Olivia and Finley had been in the same class since kindergarten. They didn't have much in common, but over the summer they'd been forced to share a cabin at sleep-away camp, and Finley had learned that Olivia wasn't so bad. They were even starting to become friends.

All around the room, students buzzed with excited chatter. Ms. Bird liked the noise level kept to a dull roar, but this was a *real* roar.

That's what happens when you put up twinkling lights and bring a robot dog to school, thought Finley.

Ms. Bird stood beside her desk and rang her magic chime, but it didn't work. Finley could barely hear it over the ruckus. Ms. Bird tried turning off the lights, but that just made things worse.

"CLASS, PLEASE TAKE YOUR SEATS!" a robotic voice boomed. Everyone went silent.

When all the students had settled down, Ms. Bird flicked the lights back on and walked to the front of the room. She cradled Tesla in one hand and held a strange-looking megaphone in the other. "The modern megaphone was invented by Thomas Edison in the late 1800s," she said in her robo-tone, "but I like this newfangled model, complete with voice modulator."

Ms. Bird set the megaphone and Tesla on her desk. "I know you're curious about what we'll be working on," she continued in her regular chirpy voice, "so put on your listening ears."

Finley *was* curious. She glanced at Henry, then put her pencil down and sat at attention.

"Our world is a wonderful place," Ms. Bird said as she drew a giant Earth on the board with a green marker. "But it has some problems, too. Luckily, there's a powerful tool we can use to solve them. Does anyone know what that tool might be?"

Finley didn't know. And from the looks of it, no one else did either.

Ms. Bird perched on her tall stool and folded her hands. She looked confident, like she knew someone was going to come up with the perfect answer at any moment. But judging by her classmates' zombie-like stares, Finley was pretty sure they weren't.

Suddenly, Olivia put up her hand and shook it like her fingers were on fire. "A smartphone!" she shrieked.

"Good guess," said Ms. Bird. "A smartphone *is* a useful tool. However, it's not the tool I have in mind."

Henry raised his hand.

Ms. Bird pointed in his direction. "Henry?"

"The electric drill?"

Ms. Bird smiled. "Electric drills are helpful, too," she said. "But the tool I'm thinking of is something everyone is born with."

Finley pictured a newborn baby holding an electric drill — that was *definitely* not something everyone was born with.

"*Think* about it," Ms. Bird said, tapping the side of her head.

I'm thinking so hard my brain hurts, Finley thought. Then it hit her. "Oh!" she blurted out. "The brain!"

Ms. Bird nodded. "Exactly. Every helpful invention, from the robot dog to the megaphone to the electric drill, started with an idea in a brain like yours. You might think, 'What good can I do? I'm just a kid.' But kids have come up with some amazing inventions."

"Like what?" asked Olivia.

"Like Popsicles," Ms. Bird said, drawing one on the board. "And earmuffs. And trampolines. I bet you'll find a lot more as you research. For our first big class project, I want each of you to design your own invention — a 'nice device' that makes the world a better place."

Ms. Bird finished drawing earmuffs and a trampoline, then added shine lines all around the Earth to show that it had been better-ified.

A kid invented Popsicles? Finley thought. *That does make the world a better place.* She wanted to invent something great, too. Something that would change the world. She raised her hand. "So how do we start?"

Chapter 2
THE NEXT PET ROCK

"Have you ever heard the saying 'necessity is the mother of invention'?" Ms. Bird asked. She strolled to the back of the classroom and paused under the giant lightbulb. "Thinking of a problem or something people need is a great first step to inventing." She pointed to a glossy poster and read, "Information + Inspiration + Imagination + Determination = Innovation."

"What in *tarnation* does that mean?" Henry whispered.

Finley shrugged. She got the "imagination" part, but she wasn't so sure about the rest.

"That means that research might inspire you to think of an interesting idea," Ms. Bird continued. "And if you stick with your idea and keep trying, you could come up with a great new thing. At the Inventor Center you can find lots of information to get you started."

She gestured to the bookshelves and the tables stacked with magazines. "We'll work on this project all week, and on Friday we'll have an Invention Convention where you'll share your creations with some special guests." She looked at Finley. "I can't wait to see what you come up with."

Me, too, thought Finley.

Olivia waved her hand in the air. "What do we get if we win?" she asked.

"It's not a contest," Ms. Bird explained, "just a chance to learn and meet some expert inventors. You'll get the satisfaction of thinking of a great new idea and sharing it."

"Oh." Olivia slouched in her chair. She looked like her enthusiasm had sprung a leak.

Expert inventors! thought Finley. *I wonder who they could be. Whoever they are, I'm going to come up with something Fin-omenal to show them. It's my first fourth-grade project, and I'm going to make a good impression!*

When Ms. Bird announced it was research time, Finley took a seat at a round table in the Inventor Center with Henry, Olivia, and their other friends, Kate and Lia. She grabbed a magazine and leafed through it. There were designs of flying cars, pictures of musical socks that played notes when you wiggled your toes, and inflatable fortune cookie balloons with messages inside them. There was even a bracelet that could be unraveled and used as dental floss.

"Cool!" said Henry, pointing to a picture in his book. "A Handlebar Mustache! It's a giant mustache that attaches to your bike handlebars. It even has pockets for snacks and drinks."

"What about this Numbrella?" said Lia. "It teaches you math while keeping you dry. It's like a pie chart. When you press different buttons on the handle, the different sections of the pie light up to show fractions."

"Look!" Finley held up her magazine. "It's Gary Dahl — the guy who invented the pet rock. It says here he's sold millions of them. He made more than fifteen million dollars in six months!"

"Selling rocks?" Kate made a face.

"*Pet* rocks," said Finley. "They come with their own special crate and training manual."

"That's ridiculous," said Olivia. "Who wants to have a rock for a pet? They don't fetch or cuddle. They don't even move."

"They can play dead and roll over," Finley pointed out. "And they don't need food or housetraining." She stared at the picture of Gary Dahl. "I want to sell millions of *my* invention. Maybe the expert inventors will tell me how. Or maybe they'll even want to buy my idea. Then I'd be rich and famous! I'd donate half my money to build the school a swimming pool and a skating rink and an awesome new art room with tons of cool supplies. And I'd get Mom and Dad a new car while I'm at it — Mom's always wanted a convertible."

"Sounds good to me," said Henry. "Now you just have to think of something to invent."

Finley stared at her blank paper. Then she flipped it over and stared at the other side. She wished she had some chocolate chips. Chocolate chips always helped her think. At least she could doodle. She took out a pencil and made a circle. She drew a line next to it, then more lines. It looked like a sun. Finley gave it a smile and sunglasses. "Major brainstorm alert!" she announced. "I've got it — glow-in-the-dark sunscreen! I'll bet you've never seen *that* before!"

"Nope," said Olivia. "Probably because people don't need sunscreen when it's dark."

"Glow-in-the-dark *moon*screen might work," Henry suggested.

"Moonscreen?" Olivia rolled her eyes. "You're a space cadet!"

Finley and her friends sat and thought. Henry wrote a column of neatly printed numbers to start an

idea list. He *loved* making lists. Olivia picked little lint balls off her sweater and rolled them into one big lint ball. Finley twirled one of the loose strands of hair that had escaped from her braids. *Maybe if I twirl hard enough*, she thought, *it'll wind up my brain*.

Finley usually had so many new ideas they squeezed out the other thoughts — the ones that helped her remember the capital of Nebraska or where she'd left her sweater. *Why is it easy to think of ideas when you don't need them and hard to think of them when you do?* she wondered.

Henry started whistling "Blue Suede Shoes" as he finished numbering his list. Henry loved Elvis. "Hey," he said, putting his pencil down. "Remember how some of the older kids at Camp Acorn whittled those twig whistles?"

Finley frowned. "Yeah, I remember. I wanted to make one, but they said I was too little to whittle."

"Well, I've got something even better — an edible whistle!" said Henry. "You could blow it, then eat it!"

"*Eat* it?" Olivia made a face.

"Uh-huh," said Henry. "You could wear it around your neck. That way you'd never leave home without a snack."

"Good idea," said Finley. "But what kind of snack could be a whistle?"

"Remember the fruit leather I made in camp cooking class?" Henry asked.

Olivia wrinkled her nose. "Don't remind us."

"I could sculpt whistles out of fruit leather," Henry said. "They could even come in different flavors."

"Yuck," said Olivia.

"You're a genius," said Finley. Ever since the school cook-off, Henry had been coming up with fun, new snacks.

Finley was glad Henry had his idea, but she was still drawing a blank. She flipped through the pages of an *Inventor's Monthly* magazine. Solar-powered water bottle fan, laser toenail clippers, mini-flower-vase barrettes, washable chalkboard doodle-pants. It was a well-known fact that making things was her thing. But could she think of an invention as great as those?

Ms. Bird rang the chime. This time everyone stopped, looked, and listened. "We'll be starting math in five minutes," she said, "so please finish up. I hope you found some interesting information — maybe even some inspiration. But if not, don't worry. Ideas are everywhere. Sometimes you can even get one by playing."

Finley put away her magazine, but she couldn't stop thinking about the Invention Convention. She knew the perfect idea was somewhere in her brain — a tiny seed ready to grow and burst into bloom. She just hoped it would hurry.

Chapter 3

IT'S ALL BEEN DONE BEFORE

When Finley got home, she ran up to her room and opened her toy chest. If Ms. Bird said ideas came from playing, then she was going to play. She took out a purple velvet bag and dug through her old marble collection. She'd forgotten how cool marbles were — how they clinked together and felt so smooth and perfect in her hand. There were big, cloudy glass ones with tiny bubbles, shiny silver steelies that were heavier than the rest, and clear ones that looked like cats' eyes with ribbons of color twisting through the centers.

Finley held an orange-and-blue marble up to the light and admired its swirly stripes. Then she rummaged through the chest and found her old superhero cape. She tied one end of the cape to the back of her desk chair and pulled the other end tight over the seat, tying it to the chair legs.

Finley rolled a marble down the slanted fabric, then flung it back up, launching it off the top of the chair just as her older brother, Zack, opened her bedroom door. The marble flew across the room and pelted him in the stomach.

"Ow!" he said. "Watch it!"

"Sorry," said Finley. "You should have knocked before entering. This is a maximum-security lab."

Zack rolled his eyes. "Mom says it's your turn to set the table. Dinner is in half an hour."

"Wait!" said Finley. "Look what I made! It's a project for school — we have to design our own invention. I call it the Superbly Slanted Slope." She motioned for Zack to move and launched another marble. "So, what do you think?"

Zack raised an eyebrow. "I think it's dangerous. And it's not your invention — it's basically an inclined plane. The ancient Egyptians used them to build the pyramids."

Finley narrowed her eyes. "Are you sure?"

"Sure, I'm sure," Zack said. "Look it up."

"I will," said Finley. "Tell Mom I'll be there in a bit."

"Fine." Zack turned and headed down the hall.

Finley sighed. She didn't have to look it up. Zack was always right about stuff like that. Plus, he'd studied ancient civilizations last year in fifth grade. She remembered his project on mummies. "Great," she mumbled. "Back to the drawing board."

Maybe there's an idea hiding in here, Finley thought as she pulled her junk trunk out of her closet. She threw open the lid and sorted through her heaping collection: a dissected clock, broken building sets, tangles of yarn, pieces of toys, sheets of half-popped Bubble Wrap, rolls of ribbon, duct tape, wrinkled foil, and mountains of paper clips and bottle caps.

Finley grabbed some supplies and set to work. She was trying to build a robot cat out of Popsicle sticks, tinfoil, and rubber bands when her fingers slipped, and its head shot across the room.

Aha! Finley thought. *Inspiration strikes!* She wrapped a rubber band around the ends of two Popsicle sticks and rolled up a long piece of tape, wedging it between the sticks so they made a *V*. Then she crunched some foil into a ball, turned the *V* on its side, set the ball on the end of the top stick, and pressed it down, ready to launch.

Just then, Zack passed by. "How do you like my Stupendous Sphere Slinger?" Finley called.

As Zack poked his head in the doorway, she slid her finger off the end of the stick, and it sprang up, sending the foil ball flying.

"Hey!" Zack yelped, as it hit him between the eyes. "You mean *catapult*? Some Greek guy made them popular more than two thousand years ago."

Finley groaned. As soon as Zack had left, she went to the computer and looked it up. There it was, her very own invention: a catapult. She was getting sick of people stealing her ideas. Even if those people had been dead for centuries.

Finley took out her sketchbook. Maybe she needed to draw up a few plans. She scribbled and labeled. Then she went back to her junk trunk and tinkered and tweaked.

"Zack!" she yelled. "Come look at this!"

"Not now!" he shouted. "I'm playing *Extreme Zombie Picnic*, and I just made it to level ten!"

"Pleeeeeeeease?"

"Oh, all right," Zack said. "But hold your fire." Finley heard him plod down the hall. He peered in, shielding his face with the video-game controller.

"Ta-daaah!" Finley said, holding up a pincer-like contraption. She opened and closed its claws with a scissoring motion and demonstrated picking up a Styrofoam ball. "Introducing the Great Gotcha Grabber!"

Zack shook his head. "Salad tongs. Listen, I don't want to burst your bubble," he said, popping a scrap of Bubble Wrap, "but why don't you just give up? Everything's already been invented."

"Give up?" Finley grabbed her pencil. "Are you kidding? Check out my Fabulous Floaty Flyer!" She pointed to a diagram in her sketchbook.

Zack shrugged. "Looks like a kite to me."

"No problem," Finley told him. "I've got more." She flipped the page. "Spectacular Stick Shooter?"

Zack sighed. "Crossbow. Ancient China."

"Deluxe Dirt Digger?" she said hopefully.

"That would be a garden hoe."

"Load-Lightening Levitator!" Finley said, her voice cracking.

Zack held the video-game controller like a microphone. "Ladies and gentlemen, I give you . . . the pulley," he said in his best TV-announcer voice, "lifting cargo and hoisting sails for thousands of years!"

"Finley Flowers, dinner's ready! Come set the table!" Mom's voice echoed down the hall.

"I'll be right there!" Finley yelled. Then she turned back to Zack. "What about the Monster Mosquito Masher?"

"Fly swatter." Zack fake-yawned. "Been there, done that. Now, are you finished? I'm hungry."

Finley swiped at him with her sketchbook as he turned to leave. "Nope," she told him. "I'm just getting started."

Chapter 4

SUPERSONIC SIBLING SUBLIMATOR

The next day at lunch, Finley was getting ready to eat her dessert first when Henry slid into the seat across from her.

"How's it going?" he asked. "Did you think of an —"

"Don't mention inventions," Finley said, taking a bite of her oatmeal cookie.

Henry frowned. "You didn't come up with anything new and good?"

Finley shook her head glumly. "Not even anything new and *bad*. Nothing's sprouting in my idea garden."

Henry pulled a plastic bag out of his backpack and took out a globby, brownish tube. "If it makes you feel any better, my Fruity Tooter is a complete failure," he said, holding it up. "The cat ate the first one before I had a chance to test it, and this one won't even make a squeak." He blew into the end to demonstrate, and the whistle let out an airy whisper.

"At least you came up with a new idea," said Finley. "All of my inventions were already invented."

"Did you know Ben Franklin invented swim fins when he was only eleven?" Henry said. "If he could do it, so can we." Henry ripped the whistle in half and handed Finley a sticky piece. "Here," he said, cramming the other half into his mouth. "At least it's tasty. I was thinking I might invent something to do with bugs. Or soccer. Or maybe a new kitchen gadget."

Just then a loud burp erupted from one of the third-grade tables.

Olivia set her tray down next to Finley's and glared in that direction. "Someone needs to teach them some manners."

"Maybe you should invent a manners machine," Finley suggested, as she chomped on her fruit leather.

"That's not a bad idea," said Olivia. "The world could use more politeness." Then she poured a cup of apple juice and took a dainty sip with her pinky stuck out.

"I wish *I* could burp like that," Henry said. "I've never been a very good burper."

"That's not something you should aspire to," said Olivia. "We're supposed to be the mature ones and set a good example, remember?"

"I can't help it," said Henry. "It's a skill I've always admired. I wouldn't do it all the time. But if I ever needed to use it, I could — kind of like karate."

"*Needed* to use it?" Olivia rolled her eyes. "When would that happen? If someone challenged you to a burp duel?"

Finley pictured Henry and a belching bandit facing off for a burp battle to the death.

Henry shrugged. "I dunno. Maybe I'd use it at the talent show. I could burp the school song in one breath."

"That might be considered inappropriate," Finley said.

"My manners machine would teach you that there *is* no appropriate time to burp," said Olivia.

Henry took a bite of his sandwich, and his eyes lit up. "Maybe I could invent a burping apparatus — something to help burp-challenged people like me."

"Or maybe not," said Olivia.

Henry ignored her and took out his notebook and pencil. "It'll take some research," he said, sketching out a rough design.

Finley sighed. "Sounds like you guys have big plans. Now *I* just have to come up with an idea."

* * *

After school Finley went straight to her room to experiment. Henry and Olivia had each thought of a problem and then come up with an invention to solve it. *So what's my problem, aside from being invention-less?* she wondered.

Finley was sitting in front of a mountain of mismatched pieces and parts when Zack poked his head in. "Hard at work again?" he said. "I think you need an invention inventor."

"Ha, ha," said Finley. "Very funny. I think *you* need to disappear."

Zack cupped a hand to his ear. "Uh-oh, homework's calling. Good luck, Einstein."

Finley leaped up and shut the door behind him. Zack was such a know-it-all. Especially now that he was in sixth grade. Big brothers were a big problem.

Hey, Finley thought. *Maybe that's it! I could invent something to keep older brothers and sisters from bugging people. Kate's older sister always borrows her skateboard without asking, and Lia's older brother lost her lucky Frisbee. Stuff like that happens all the time. If I could stop it, that would be a great service to humanity.*

Finley spent the rest of the afternoon in her room, drawing, tying, taping, gluing, and building the most useful Fin-vention ever. She was lying on her bed, exhausted, when Zack knocked on the door.

"What was all that racket?" he said. "Where did all of your not-inventions go? And what is that?" He pointed at the chair in the middle of the floor that was rigged up with levers, pulleys, buttons, and a tangle of attachments.

"If you *must* know," said Finley, "I combined my other ideas into an outstandingly original, incredibly ingenious invention."

"Oh, yeah?" Zack said. "What is it?"

"I call it the Supersonic Sibling Sublimator," said Finley.

"That's a mouthful," Zack said, smirking. "What does it do?"

"It sublimates siblings," said Finley. "Older ones, specifically."

"Really?" said Zack. "Sublimates — as in changes them from a solid to a gas?"

"Poof!" Finley snapped her fingers. "Just like that. It's never been done before, and it will make the world a better place."

"Well, what are you waiting for?" Zack picked his way across the mess on the floor. "One sibling at your service. Sign me up — let's test this thing out."

"Are you sure?" Finley asked.

"Absolutely," Zack said. "Let's take it for a spin."

Finley frowned. "Okay, but don't you want to say goodbye to Mom and Dad? I don't know exactly what'll happen once you're sublimated."

Zack shook his head. "You can tell them for me. Besides, can't you just reverse the process and bring me back?"

"Sure," said Finley, trying to sound convincing. "I mean, I *think* I can —"

"I *know* you can," Zack said. "I believe in you." He pointed to the chair. "Is this where I'm supposed to sit?"

Finley nodded.

Zack sat in the chair and looked at her expectantly.

Finley placed a bike helmet with a tinfoil antenna on his head. Suddenly, she was feeling a little queasy. Maybe this wasn't such a great idea after all. Zack was an enormous pain, but did he deserve to be sublimated? "Are you one hundred percent positive about this?" she asked.

Zack adjusted the helmet and gave Finley a cheery thumbs-up. "Ready when you are!"

"Well," Finley said, "good luck." She shook his hand, took a deep breath, and pressed a red button.

Nothing happened.

She tried again. Still nothing.

"Fiddlesticks," she said. "I think it might need a few minor adjustments."

"No worries." Zack grabbed a comic book and propped his feet up on Finley's desk. "Adjust away.

I've got plenty of time. Mom said I can't go anywhere until my homework is done."

Finley crawled around on the floor, tweaking levers and tightening screws. "Almost ready," she said, double-checking her diagrams. "Just one more minute."

Finley finished fine-tuning and did a final inspection. But when she turned around, the chair was empty.

Chapter 5
BRAND-NEW THING

The only trace of Zack was the comic he'd been reading, which now lay on the floor beside the Sublimator. His helmet sat on the chair like an empty shell.

"Great," Finley muttered. "He had one job — to sit in the chair. And somehow he managed to mess it up."

Finley stuck her head into the hallway. "Zack!" she called. "Come back! It's ready!"

There was no reply.

Finley tiptoed down the hall to Zack's room. She could hear the theme song for *Extreme Zombie Picnic*, but when she peeked in, he wasn't there.

She checked the bathroom.

"Zack!" she yelled again.

Finley searched every room in the house, but Zack was nowhere to be found.

Could it be? she thought. *Has he really been sublimated?* Suddenly, she felt all cold and clammy. Her throat tightened, and her stomach got that awful, carsick feeling.

It was almost dinnertime, and Finley was getting desperate. She slunk into the kitchen. "Mom, Dad, have you seen Zack?" she asked, trying to keep her voice sounding breezy.

"Not lately," said Mom.

Finley swallowed hard. "Well, I really need to find him."

"He's around," said Dad. "He was up in his room playing *Extreme Zombie* —"

"I know," Finley said. "Thanks."

Finley ran outside and checked the backyard. *"Za-aaack!"* she shouted. But the only answer was the frantic barking of the yippy dog two doors down and the wail of a distant siren.

At six o'clock, Zack still hadn't turned up. He never missed his favorite show, *Dumb Things People Do to Get on TV,* which would be starting any minute. Finley's stomach sank. It was obvious. Her invention had worked: her sibling had been sublimated.

Finley sprinted to her room. *Pull yourself together,* she thought. *You're the one who sent him away. Surely, you can bring him back.* She re-adjusted every part of the machine. She checked the connections. Then she reversed all the levers and pushed the red button.

Finley counted to ten.

Still no Zack.

She knew what she had to do, and it wasn't going to be easy.

Finley flew downstairs and burst into the kitchen. Her seven-year-old sister, Evie — a big fan of all things spooky — was reading her *Haunted Homes & Gardens* magazine, and Mom and Dad were busy cooking. They looked so normal. So happy. So unsuspecting. Not like people whose only son had just been zapped into nothingness by their very own daughter.

Savor these last blissful moments of ignorance, Finley thought. Then she gathered up her courage. "Hey, Mom," she said. "Hey, Dad."

Mom stirred a pot on the stove. "Hi, honey. What's up?" she said without turning around.

"Um . . . kind of a lot." Finley cleared her throat. "It's about Zack."

"What did he do now?" Dad asked as he rummaged around in the fridge.

"Well, actually nothing," Finley replied. "He was helping me with a project for school, and —"

"That's great," Mom said. "I've noticed you two have been making a real effort to get along lately."

Finley sighed. There was no easy way to break the news. She'd have to just come right out and say it. She took a big breath. "Zack's disappeared, and it's all my fault. I zapped him with my Supersonic Sibling Sublimator, and he's gone forever, and I'm so, so sorry!" Tears filled her eyes, and she ran out of the kitchen.

As she turned the corner into the living room, Finley tripped over something big and plowed into the coffee table, banging her knee. She looked back to see Zack rolling on the rug, laughing hysterically.

"*Ba-ha-haa-haaaaa!* I can't believe you fell for that!" he said between gasps. "I've been following you around this whole time!"

Finley froze. Her cheeks flamed. Suddenly, she was sorry he hadn't been sublimated. "Oooh!" she said, pointing a finger at him. "Just wait till I get that thing working!" Then she gave him a final glare and stomped upstairs.

Finley was lying on her bed, plotting revenge, when Zack pushed her door open a crack and peeked in.

"Out!" she yelled. "Out! Out! Out!"

"Aw, lighten up," Zack said. "Mom and Dad said I had to come apologize. I was just joking. You need to learn how to laugh things off."

"Easy for you to say," Finley said, pouting. "You aren't the one who thought you permanently disappeared someone. And you don't have a big invention project due in three days and nothing to show for it."

Zack shrugged. "If you want, I can pretend to disappear again. Then you can say your invention worked. And *I* could miss school."

Finley shook her head. "But it *doesn't* work. That wouldn't be helping anyone. And that's the whole point of the project."

"It'd be helping *me*," said Zack. "I have a math test Friday."

"No thanks," said Finley. "I need a brand-new thing. I have to come up with another invention that actually works."

"Suit yourself," said Zack, turning to go. "But remember my offer. I'd much rather be sublimated than take that test."

Finley sighed. She'd thought the Invention Convention was going to be fun, but it was turning out to be a real fun-fail. Coming up with a million-dollar idea was seriously stressful. Zack was right about one thing — she could use a good laugh.

Wait a minute! Finley thought, sitting up straight in bed. *That's it!*

She ran to the computer and did a quick search. Then she grabbed her sketchbook.

Chapter 6

JOY TO THE WORLD

The next morning, Ms. Bird gave the class extra free time before recess. Finley, Henry, and Olivia raced over to the Inventor Center.

"The week's half over, but I finally have an idea," said Finley. "And this time it's going to work!"

"I knew you'd think of something," Henry said. "Your idea-sprouting Flower Power never fails. So, what is it?"

"I'm going to invent a laugh machine to bring joy to the world!" Finley announced.

"*Joooy tooo the wooorld!*" Henry sang. "Sounds like a plan."

"How does it work?" Olivia asked.

"I haven't exactly figured that part out yet," Finley admitted. "But I did some research, just like Ms. Bird said, and I discovered that laughing is healthy — studies show it can even help you live longer."

"Wow!" said Henry. "Laughing is serious."

"I guess laughter really is the best medicine," said Olivia.

Finley nodded. "My machine is going to help people live longer and have fun doing it," she said. "All I have to do is figure out how to make them laugh."

"That's easy," Henry said. "Jokes!"

"Good idea! You're the joke expert," said Finley. "Want to help me come up with some?"

"Okey-jokey," Henry said. "We'll make a list — knock-knocks, riddles — anything *pun*-ny!"

"Great!" Finley said. "We can write down all your best ones, then I'll put them together into a joke book and attach it to my invention."

"So what's the rest of your invention?" Olivia asked.

"I don't know yet," said Finley. "I'm making it up as I go. So far it's just a cardboard box with the words *LaughCrafter* printed on the side."

"Jokes are a great start for a laugh machine," Henry said. "Guess what? I found out that *burps* are good for you, too."

Olivia narrowed her eyes at him. "No, they're not."

Henry nodded. "It's true. When you swallow food and drink, air goes down with them. If the air gets trapped in there, it can make you feel sick. So you've got to let it out — in the form of a burp!"

"What if you don't *want* to burp?" Olivia asked.

Henry shrugged. "I guess you could hold it. But it'd come out in the end."

"Ha, ha!" Finley laughed. "The *end*!"

"A burp is but a bit of wind that cometh from the heart," said Henry. "But when it takes the downward route, it cometh as a —"

"Gross!" Olivia made a face.

"Makes burping sound a lot more appealing, doesn't it?" Henry grinned, dimples creasing his cheeks.

"You're not really making some kind of burp device for the Invention Convention, are you?" Olivia wrinkled her nose.

"Why not?" said Henry. "It will improve life for people who have trouble burping. It's almost finished. I call it . . . The Burpolator."

"What do you think Ms. Bird will think of The Burpolator?" Olivia asked.

"Once she hears my presentation, she'll probably want to try it out," said Henry.

Finley pictured Ms. Bird burping. "Ms. Burp," she said. "Now *that's* funny. But seriously, I need some jokes."

"Okay," said Henry. "What did the digital clock say to the grandfather clock?"

"I dunno," said Finley.

"Look, grandpa — no hands!" Henry held his hands up.

"Ha!" said Finley. "Good one!"

"Don't you worry," Henry told her. "We'll have those experts rolling on the floor."

Finley smiled to herself. This was going to be her Fin-niest creation yet!

Chapter 7
SENSE-OF-HUMOR TEST

After school, Finley made a book out of notebook paper and bound it with swirly-patterned duct tape. She copied down the list of jokes Henry had given her and wrote "READ ME" on the cover.

"Time to test out LaughCrafter attachment number one," she said, flipping through the pages.

Finley ran downstairs to her parents' home office. Mom was sitting at the computer, writing. "Hey, Mom," Finley said, "why do spiders use computers?"

"Hmmm?" Mom mumbled without looking up.

Finley didn't wait for an answer. "To build their websites! Get it?"

"Mm-hmm . . ." Mom's fingers kept tapping out a rhythm on the keyboard.

"Never mind," Finley said under her breath. Mom probably wasn't the best test subject anyway. She always thought things were funny that weren't funny and didn't laugh at things that were.

Finley headed to the kitchen next. She found Dad making his famous Scottish black lasagna, which was known for its overcooked, extra-crunchy top. "Knock, knock!" she said.

"Come on in," Dad said, spooning sauce into a casserole dish.

"No, *knock, knock*."

Dad glanced up, a limp lasagna noodle in hand.

"Who's there?" Finley hinted.

"Oh!" said Dad. "Who's there?"

"Hatch."

"Hatch who?" Dad said.

"Bless you!" Finley grinned.

"Nice one," said Dad.

Finley frowned. "I thought it was funny."

"It *is* funny," Dad said as he sprinkled cheese on the noodles.

"Then why aren't you laughing?"

Dad looked at Finley. "I don't know," he said. "I guess something really has to tickle my funny bone to make me laugh out loud. That was a good one, though. Very clever."

"Thanks," Finley muttered. Then she left him to his lasagna.

In the living room, Evie had spread out her dolls on the floor and was painting Cute Little Cupcake's hair with green nail polish.

"What are you doing?" Finley asked.

"Spookifying my dolls," Evie said. "They're much more interesting that way. What are you doing?"

"Working on my invention project for school," said Finley. "Hey, speaking of spooky, where do little ghosts sit on car trips?"

"Beats me," Evie said.

"Boo-ster seats!"

"Har, har," said Evie, carefully applying another coat of green goo to Cupcake's curls.

Finley flipped to a new page in her joke book. "Where do spirits shop?"

"The ghostery store?" Evie guessed.

"Um . . . yeah," said Finley. "Funny, right?"

"Yeah," Evie echoed. "Funny."

"But this is *really* funny — why didn't the ghost pass the test?"

Evie shrugged.

"Because he didn't believe in himself," said Finley. "Get it?"

Evie shook her head. "Not really," she said. "Hey, why all the jokes? What is this?"

"It's a sense-of-humor test," said Finley, "and you just failed it."

Finley turned and stomped back up to her room. She hated to admit it, but *she* was the one who'd failed. *People laugh all the time*, she thought. *So why is it so hard to make them?*

Chapter 8
JUST FOR LAUGHS

Finley grabbed her sketchbook off her bed. *I need better jokes*, she thought. *Some guaranteed giggle-getters.*

When Finley went back downstairs, Evie was camped out in front of the TV. *The Mew Crew* was one of Evie's favorite shows, although Finley couldn't see why. It was about a bunch of talking cats that ran around their neighborhood helping pets in trouble. It wasn't even funny, but sometimes Evie laughed so hard Finley thought she might hyperventilate.

As Finley watched, one of the cats on the show knocked over a glass of milk, and five kittens came pitter-pattering to drink it. Evie burst into hysterical giggles.

"What's so hilarious about that?" Finley asked.

Evie shrugged. "I dunno. It just *is*. Listen — everyone else is laughing, too."

Finley listened. Sure enough, a wave of laughter swept over the invisible TV audience.

"Those aren't real people," Zack said as he passed by with a tray of snacks. "They're canned laughs."

"Canned laughs?" Evie scrunched up her nose.

"Also known as a laugh track," Zack said. "It's a recording of people laughing. They play it after the jokes to make you think they're funny."

"Huh," Evie said. "It works."

"But that's cheating," said Finley. "The laughs are fake."

"It doesn't matter." Zack nodded at Evie. "Look at her."

As if to prove his point, Evie erupted in another giggle fit.

"Laughs are contagious," Zack explained. "Hearing them makes people laugh. TV shows are just using that to their advantage." He turned and headed upstairs.

Huh, Finley thought. *Maybe I don't need better jokes after all. Maybe I need canned laughs.*

She ran to her room and got her mini voice recorder. Then she plopped down on the floor and scooted in close to Evie. As soon as Evie started giggling, Finley pressed record. After a couple of minutes, she had plenty of homemade canned laughs. *It's only Evie*, she thought. *But maybe I can sample some more.*

Finley tiptoed upstairs and down the hall to Zack's room. She dropped to her hands and knees and peered through the door. Zack's friend Sam had come over to play video games, and they were in the middle of an intergalactic space battle. Finley crept up behind Zack's chair.

Suddenly, he spun around to face her. "What are you doing in my room?" he demanded.

"Nothing," Finley said, hiding the recorder behind her back.

"Nothing?" Zack put out his hand and made a give-it-here motion with his fingers.

Finley sighed. Busted. She passed him the recorder. "I'm just trying to catch some laughs."

Zack raised an eyebrow. "You're recording them?"

Finley nodded. "It's my own laugh library. I'm going to use it as a canned-laughs attachment for my invention. If you let me record yours, you guys will be famous, and you'll be helping millions of people live longer, happier lives. Plus, you owe me one after your disappearing act."

Zach grinned. "We'll give it our best, then."

Zack and Sam exchanged looks, then exploded into laughter.

"BAAA-HA-HAAA! HEEE-HEEEEEE-HOOO!"

"A-HAHAHAHAHAHAHAAAA!"

"TEEEE-HE-HEEEE!"

"HOOOO-EEEEE!"

"Thanks," Finley said. "That'll do."

"*N-YUK, N-YUK, N-YUK!*"

"*HEEE-HEEEE! HA-HA-HA-HAAAA!*"

Finley covered her ears. "ALL RIGHT!" she yelled. "THAT'S GOOD, THANKS!"

"No problem," Zack said, taking a bow. "We're here to help."

* * *

It took her a while, but Finley managed to capture a good collection of laughs. Dad had two types: a cheerful, clucking chuckle and a knee-slapping wheeze that left him gasping for air. Evie did her standard giggle-and-shriek. And Mom's high-pitched cackle erupted suddenly like a volcano.

The more Finley thought about it, the more she realized that laughs were mysterious. Somehow, they popped up out of nowhere and took over.

When Henry really got going, he made a noise like a barking seal. Once Kate had laughed so hard she'd peed her pants. And another time in the lunchroom, Henry had told a joke, and Finley had spewed chocolate milk out her nose. That part hadn't been so funny — especially to the lunchroom supervisor.

Whatever laughs were, Finley hoped that once the experts heard them, they wouldn't be able to resist joining in. Clearly, everyone had different funny bones, so the more LaughCrafter attachments, the better. Right now all she had was a cardboard box holding a joke book and canned laughs. Finley planned to keep her eyes peeled for anything else remotely hilarious. She was going funny hunting.

Chapter 9

FUNNY FACE

The next morning, Finley went to school armed with her sketchbook and a pencil. She had one more day till the Invention Convention. It was time to get serious.

All through math, Finley was alert and ready for when something funny came her way. Unfortunately, nothing did — just plain old decimals and word problems about people buying fruit and taking boring car trips to visit their grandma in Indiana. Silent reading was the same. It didn't help that her book was on the Boston Tea Party, which turned out to be way less fun than it sounded.

At snack time, Finley was washing her hands in the classroom sink, daydreaming about what color convertible she'd buy after selling her invention, when she caught a glimpse of her crooked reflection in the faucet. Her head was bulging, her eyes were buggy, and her nose looked like a huge hot dog with freckles.

Now, that's funny, Finley thought. She ran to get Henry.

"Check it out," she said, pointing to the faucet. "It messes up your face."

Henry leaned in for a closer look. "Cool!" he said. "It's like a funhouse mirror."

"Maybe I can add it to the LaughCrafter," said Finley. "A funny-face attachment would be perfect!"

Finley and Henry tried making different faces. They crossed their eyes and did fishy lips. They stuck out their tongues and puffed up their cheeks. They pretended to be aliens. "Take me to your leader," they said, waving their arms around. They were so busy cracking up, they didn't notice Olivia watching.

"What are you guys doing?" she asked.

Finley had her fingers hooked in the sides of her mouth. She turned to face Olivia. "Wesearch!" she said. "Twy it! Iff fum!"

"Fum?" Olivia echoed.

Finley took her fingers out of her mouth. *"Fun.* We're researching funny things for my invention," she explained, pointing to the reflection. "Look — your face is all warped."

"You're warped," Olivia said, peering into the faucet. "Yikes! That's going to give me bad dreams."

"I'm going to add it to the LaughCrafter," Finley said as they all headed back to the snack table.

"How are you going to attach it?" Olivia asked. "You can't bring the whole sink."

Finley frowned. "True . . ."

"You need something more portable," Henry said, opening his applesauce. "What else is curved and shiny?"

"Spoons!" Finley said, pointing to the one in Henry's hand.

Olivia shook her head. "Not big enough."

"Hubcaps!" said Henry.

Olivia rolled her eyes. "*Too* big. Plus, where is she going to get a hubcap by tomorrow?"

Henry shrugged. "She could borrow one off a car."

"Not worth the jail time," Olivia said, nibbling her granola bar. "What about mixing bowls?"

"Our mixing bowls are glass," said Finley.

"You can use one of our metal ones," Henry offered. "Mom and Dad never do. I can drop it off on the way to soccer."

"Thanks," said Finley. "Now I've got three attachments: a joke book, canned laughs, and a funny-face-maker."

"Well, I've already finished my invention," Olivia said, pulling out her sparkly purple notebook. "Check it out — here's a sketch."

Finley stared at the picture. It looked like Evie's hairdressing doll — the one that was just a big head so you could style its hair. Evie had turned hers into Medusa by coloring the hair with black marker and gluing plastic snakes on it, but the one in Olivia's sketch had a hair bow and perfect blond ringlets.

"Meet Miss Manners," said Olivia. "She can help you remember which fork to use first, teach you to say 'excuse me' in five languages, and give directions for writing a proper thank-you letter."

"Wow," said Henry. "How does she work?"

"First, you decide which manners question you need help with," Olivia explained. "Then you press the button, and Miss Manners recites the answer. Well, she doesn't really — she's actually an old Salon Style Doll. I made a recording of my voice answering each question. Here — you pick a question, and I'll pretend to be Miss Manners."

"Hmm . . ." said Henry. "I've always wondered how to tie a bowtie, or what to say if I meet the Queen. Can Miss Manners tell me that?"

Olivia sighed. "No. You have to pick one of the questions printed on the display." She pointed to the diagram in her notebook.

"What about this one?" said Finley. "Where should you put your napkin when you're eating?" She pressed the button next to the question.

"Miss Manners says, 'In your lap,'" Olivia recited in a syrupy-sweet voice.

"I usually stuff mine in the front of my shirt," said Henry. "Like a bib."

Olivia rolled her eyes. "Why am I not surprised?"

"There's just one problem with Miss Manners," said Henry. "People all over the world do things differently. In some cultures, it's even polite to burp. It tells people you enjoyed your meal. I can't wait to show you The Burpolator. It's going to help a lot of burp-less people."

"Miss Manners still says *no burping*," said Olivia. Then she drew a "NO BURPING" sign beside Miss Manners's head in her notebook.

"The cool thing about laughing is that everyone does it," said Finley. "All around the world, babies start laughing when they're only a few months old. So my invention can be used anywhere."

"Everyone can learn to burp, too," said Henry. "It's completely natural."

"A lot of things are completely natural," said Olivia. "But that doesn't mean they're polite."

"Hopefully the visitors will like all of our inventions," said Finley. "Maybe they'll even want to buy them. We'll make the world a better place and make millions at the same time!"

"Bring on the experts!" Olivia announced. "I'm ready for tomorrow!"

Finley was not so ready. She liked the idea of the LaughCrafter, but it didn't seem finished just yet. *Jokes and canned laughs and funny faces aren't enough*, she thought. *I need something more. Something stronger. But what?*

Chapter 10
TICKLE TIME

After school, Finley was sitting at the kitchen table, staring at her reflection in the mixing bowl Henry had brought her. Mom walked by with a basket of laundry and stopped to sample a spoonful of soup from the pot on the stove. "Why so glum, chum?" she asked. "Is something wrong?"

Finley sighed. "The Invention Convention is tomorrow, and I'm trying to come up with things that tickle people's funny bones." Her eyes widened. "*Tickles!* Why didn't I think of that before?"

"Your dad's feet are so ticklish, he can't go barefoot on the lawn," Mom said.

Wow, Finley thought. Come to think of it, she'd never seen him walk on the grass without shoes. And Henry was super ticklish, too.

"Thanks, Mom!" Finley ran to her room, taking the stairs two at a time. *This is great!* she thought. *Tickles are the ticket!*

Finley pulled her craft box out from under her bed and dug through a bag of multi-colored feathers. She picked out an extra-fuzzy one, tugged off her sock, and tested it on her toes. It felt weird — kind of annoying, but not tickly.

"What are you doing?" Evie asked, peeking in the half-open door.

"Trying to make a toe-tickler attachment for my laugh machine," Finley told her. "But I don't think it works."

"It's hard to tickle yourself," Evie said. "Here, let me help."

Finley stuck out her foot, and Evie swept the feather back and forth along Finley's toes. Nothing happened.

"Huh," Evie said. "Maybe you're not ticklish." She tried it on herself and burst into giggles. "But I am!"

"So is Dad," said Finley. "You must have gotten it from him." She shook the rest of the feathers out of the bag and watched them drift down like rainbow snow. "At least it works on someone."

It would be best if the special guests didn't have to tickle themselves, Finley decided. It seemed like an important part of tickling was having it done to you by someone else. But she couldn't ask them to tickle each other. She needed a tickling tool.

Finley searched the basement and dug up Zack's old hamster's cage. She pulled off the lid and took out the hamster wheel, then snuck back upstairs. It had been three years since Hank the hamster had escaped into the weedy woods that bordered the backyard. Surely Zack wouldn't mind her putting the toy to good use.

Finley taped feathers all around the outside of the wheel so they stood up like a fluffy forest of tickly trees. Then she duct taped the wheel to the top of the LaughCrafter and called Evie back to her room.

"All right," Finley said, "let's see if it works."

Evie spun the wheel and held her foot so the feathers brushed the bottom. She giggled and wiggled her toes. "It works!" she shrieked. "You try!" Then she spun the wheel again.

Finley held her foot up and let the feathers graze it. *Funny*, she thought, *but not laugh-out-loud funny.* "I dunno," she said. "I think I need a back-up plan."

"You've already got the jokes, the canned laughs, the funny-face-maker, *and* the toe-tickler," Evie reminded her.

Finley smiled. "I guess you're right. I've got Plans A, B, C, and D. The LaughCrafter is sure to be E for 'excellent!'"

Chapter 11
TOTALLY TONGUE-TIED

On Friday morning, Ms. Bird stood outside the classroom door, greeting the students as they arrived. "Welcome to the Invention Convention!" she said. "Get ready to show us your ingenious ideas!"

Finley, Henry, and Olivia lugged their stuff to their desks and started assembling their inventions. Finley couldn't wait to demonstrate the LaughCrafter. She smiled to herself as she unpacked the attachments and instruction sheets. Then she secured the funny-face-maker to the side of the box with duct tape.

Fame and fortune, here I come! she thought as she gave the toe-tickler a quick spin.

All over the room, students were setting up their nice devices. Every desk displayed a different doodad, gizmo, or thingamajig. *The world is about to be better-ified*, Finley thought, *starting right here at Glendale Elementary.*

Henry took The Burpolator out of its box and uncoiled the plastic tubes that hung from its lid. "Get ready for some beautiful belches!" he announced.

"Whoa," Finley said, "that's a cool contraption!"

"Interesting," said Olivia.

Henry beamed. "Just wait till you see it in action."

Olivia draped a purple tablecloth over her desk and arranged Miss Manners and her accessories on lace doilies. She added a model place setting and a bouquet of fake flowers. Then she put on her white gloves and a ribbon-y, wide-brimmed hat. When she was done, it looked like she and Miss Manners were having tea for two.

Just as everyone finished setting up, the visitors arrived. "Attention please!" Ms. Bird called. "I'd like to introduce our special guests. This is Mr. Wingnutt." She gestured to a balding man with a gray mustache and beard. "He's an aerospace engineer. He's designed many things, most recently some special panels for the International Space Station."

Mr. Wingnutt nodded.

"Gallopin' galaxies," Henry said under his breath.

"Next to him is Dr. Clunk," Ms. Bird continued, "President of Clunk Industries. She invented the collapsible toilet plunger." Dr. Clunk clutched her clipboard and surveyed the class like she was observing a new species of animal. She looked seriously serious. Finley wondered if she had a funny bone in her body.

"Sheesh," Henry muttered. "She should have invented a better name."

"Finally," Ms. Bird went on, "this is Mr. Quackenbottom, inventor of the world's first coffee filters made from recycled elephant dung."

"Really?" Finley whispered to Henry, her eyes wide.

"Gross!" Henry made a face.

Mr. Quackenbottom gave a nervous smile and a wave.

"These experts are all very excited to be here at our fourth-grade Invention Convention!" Ms. Bird said, clasping her hands together. "They can't wait to see your inventions in action!"

Yikes, thought Finley. *If that's what excited looks like, I'd hate to see calm.*

"Our visitors will be coming around to test out your inventions one by one," Ms. Bird explained, "so please be ready to demonstrate your device when it's your turn. After the Invention Convention is over, you'll get written feedback about your creations. Remember, we're all here to learn — so just have fun with it."

"I sure hope the LaughCrafter works," Finley whispered to Henry. "The special guests look like they could use a laugh."

Mr. Wingnutt, Dr. Clunk, and Mr. Quackenbottom walked to the end of the row, clipboards and pens poised.

First up was a boy named Arpin. He'd invented flavored snow paint.

"It's just drink mix and water in a spray bottle," Olivia whispered to Finley and Henry.

"I think it's cool," said Henry. "Now you can eat the yellow snow."

Next in line was Lia with her Hammock Hairband. "I wove it out of really thin yarn," she explained. "It unwinds and transforms into a hammock in case you're stuck somewhere and need an emergency nap."

"Wow," said Finley. "My dad could use one of those."

"Hey, there's Will," said Henry, pointing to the far side of the room. "I really want to check out his Reusable Space Candy. He told me about it at soccer practice. It's part gum, part candy, and it lasts a super-long time so you can use it again and again. Wanna come?"

"You two go ahead," said Olivia. "Gum's not my thing. My mom says it's impolite and that chewing it makes you look like a cow."

"Moo!" said Finley.

"Okay," Henry said. "We'll be right back. Just give a wave if it's our turn."

Finley followed Henry over to Will's desk.

"Mind if we sample some gum?" Henry asked.

"Sure, go ahead," said Will. "You'll be the first to try it — besides me, of course. But I only took a tiny taste." He held up a sticky, grayish hunk. "Ready to go where no kids have gone before?"

"Cool!" said Henry. "It looks like an asteroid." He took the glob and popped it into his mouth.

"Thanks," said Finley, biting off a chunk of hers. She started to chew, but as soon as the gum hit her tongue, it hardened up. It was tough, gritty, and chalky, with a hint of fake strawberry flavor. She tried to blow a bubble, but it stuck to the back of her teeth.

It looked like Henry was having the same problem. His brow furrowed as he worked his jaw from side to side. "Iff tuck," he said to Will.

"What?" Will leaned in closer.

"*Iff tuck.*" Henry pointed to his mouth. "*Elp.*"

Finley looked at the remaining candy in her hand. She tried to shake it off into the trash, but it clung to her fingers like crazy glue.

"Wha di doo pook un dere?" she asked Will.

"Huh?" said Will.

"Un *dere*," Finley said, pointing to the "Reusable Space Candy" sign on his desk.

"Oh!" Will said. "What did I put in there?"

Finley nodded.

"I can't tell you," Will said. "It's my secret formula."

Henry's eyes were bugging out, and the crinkles in his forehead had deepened into creases of concern.

"It's nothing bad," Will assured them. "It's all edible. At least I *think* it is."

Finley poked and prodded the candy with her tongue, but it wouldn't budge. As she watched the experts asking questions and making notes, her stomach got a jittery-skittery feeling. Soon it would be her turn, and she was totally tongue-tied.

Olivia was up next. Finley and Henry looked on as she held out her poofy purple dress and curtsied politely, then showed off her model place setting, complete with salad fork, bread-and-butter plate, teacup and saucer, and a big red sign that said "NO BURPING."

Mr. Wingnutt, Dr. Clunk, and Mr. Quackenbottom watched as Olivia demonstrated her invention. They pushed buttons and listened as Miss Manners gave them advice, which they hastily jotted down like they were taking a test. Push, scribble. Push, scribble. Finally, they shook Olivia's white-gloved hand, practicing her firm-and-friendly handshake technique. Then they moved on to Henry's desk.

Olivia glanced over at Finley and Henry and waved her hands like she was drowning. Henry waved back and gave her the hold-on-just-one-minute signal.

Finley and Henry pulled and pried, but they couldn't dislodge the Reusable Space Candy. As she tugged and twisted the alien gum, Finley spotted Principal Small talking to Ms. Bird by the classroom door.

Finley always felt like Principal Small was watching her, and it made her nervous. It had started in kindergarten after the Play-Doh-in-the-toilet incident and had gotten worse last year after Principal Small had sampled Finley's super-spicy PB&J Pasta at the school cook-off.

Great, thought Finley. *She must have dropped in to see the convention. Clearly, this is not a good time to ask Ms. Bird for help.*

Chapter 12

GIVE BURPS A CHANCE

"It's your turn," Will said, pointing to Henry's desk.

"We mow dat!" Henry answered. He turned to Finley. "Cub od. Weff go!"

Finley and Henry made a beeline for their desks.

Olivia met them halfway across the room. "What is wrong with you guys?" she whispered. "Hurry up!"

"Mouff tuck," Henry said. Then he pointed toward his invention. "Oo elp?"

"What?" said Olivia. "Quit joking around — it's your turn!"

Henry shook his head. "Uh-uh. Mouff tuck. Bat tandy. Elp?"

Olivia shrugged. "I don't know what you're talking about!"

Finley grabbed a pencil from the desk beside her. She jotted down a note in her sketchbook and handed it to Olivia.

"Mouth stuck," Olivia read. "Bad candy. Help?"

Finley pointed to Henry's invention.

Olivia turned to Henry. "Are you kidding? You want *me* to demonstrate The Burpolator?"

Henry nodded, looking pitiful. "I oh oo bid," he said with his best lost-puppy eyes. Then he held out his notecards.

Finley grabbed her sketchbook back from Olivia and wrote: *He'll owe you big.*

Olivia read the note and rolled her eyes. Then she smoothed out her dress, straightened her hair bow, took Henry's notecards, and marched over to his desk just as the experts were starting to move on.

"Welcome!" Olivia said to the visitors. "Remember me — Olivia Snotham, the inventor of the marvelous Miss Manners? Well, I'm also Henry Lin's assistant. He's kind of speechless at the moment, so I'll be helping demonstrate his invention."

Olivia leafed through Henry's notecards, then shoved them into the pocket of her dress. She took a deep breath, cleared her throat, and held her head high. "Have you ever wanted to be a brilliant burper?" she began. "Have you ever wondered what it would be like to produce loud, satisfying, powerful belches?"

Henry looked at Finley, his eyes wide.

The experts exchanged worried glances. "Not really," said Mr. Wingnutt.

"Well," Olivia continued, unfazed, "The Burpolator can help you do just that." She patted Henry's invention — a giant cooler with plastic tubes coming out of it. "According to doctors, holding in burps can result in uncomfortable bloating, also known as tummy troubles. With The Burpolator, you can let it all out. So," she gave the experts her best mysterious look, "who's going first?"

Mr. Wingnutt and Dr. Clunk stepped back.

"Great," Olivia said, passing Mr. Quackenbottom one of the tubes that was dangling from the cooler. "It looks like you're the lucky one. The first step is . . ." She paused to read the instruction booklet on Henry's desk. "Take a long, refreshing, bubbly drink. Don't be shy — the bigger the drink, the more effective The Burpolator will be."

Mr. Quackenbottom examined the tube. "Is that really necessary?" he asked.

"I'm afraid so," said Olivia. "Look — it's so easy, even a kid can do it." She grabbed one of the plastic tubes and took a long drink. "Mmm. See? Now it's your turn."

Mr. Quackenbottom put the tube to his mouth, and took a tiny sip.

Olivia looked at Henry, who shook his head.

"It's going to take more than that," Olivia told Mr. Quackenbottom. "Pretend you're in the middle of the Sahara Desert. You're parched like a sad, dried-up little raisin. This is your first drink in days."

Mr. Quackenbottom hesitated, then guzzled down some of the liquid.

"Well done!" said Olivia. She checked the instruction booklet. "Next — jog in place for twenty seconds." She looked at her watch. "Ready . . . set . . . go!"

Olivia started jogging.

Mr. Quackenbottom just stood there, perplexed.

"If you don't do it, we'll have to start all over," Olivia warned.

Mr. Quackenbottom jogged in place.

"Okay, stop!" Olivia said twenty seconds later. "Time for the jumping jacks. Give me ten."

Mr. Quackenbottom glanced anxiously at Mr. Wingnutt and Dr. Clunk, then followed Olivia's directions.

"Now, relax and let it *aaalllll ooooout*," Olivia instructed.

Finley looked at Henry in amazement. Olivia was like one of those salespeople on TV.

Mr. Quackenbottom did not look relaxed.

"Close your eyes and visualize *biiiig* burps," Olivia coached.

Mr. Quackenbottom closed his eyes.

"Try opening your mouth just a bit," Olivia said.

Mr. Quackenbottom opened his mouth, but nothing came out.

"Huh," said Olivia. "I don't know why it's not working. The Burpolator has never failed before. Maybe someone else should try." She looked at Mr. Wingnutt.

Mr. Wingnutt glanced at Dr. Clunk. "Actually," he said briskly, "that's all the time we have for now."

Henry grabbed Finley's sketchbook and wrote: *Give burps a chance.* But the experts were already moving on to Finley's desk and were too busy writing their own notes to see.

Finley's stomach lurched. There was no way she could demonstrate the LaughCrafter with her mouth full of Reusable Space Candy. She had to act fast. She wasn't about to let some dumb gum prevent her from bringing joy to the world.

Chapter 13
A JOYFUL NOISE

Finley clawed at the roof of her mouth and scraped her nails against the back of her teeth. Then she hooked her finger around the Reusable Space Candy and yanked as hard as she could. It stretched as Finley struggled to keep a grip, but she kept pulling.

Suddenly, there was a sucking sound — followed by a loud *pop!* — as a big gob of gum flew out of Finley's mouth and landed right in the middle of Olivia's fake flower bouquet.

Finley took a deep breath. She was free. And just in time.

She tiptoed over to Olivia's desk and gently fished the Reusable Space Candy out of the flowers. Then she smushed it between two pages of her sketchbook and stuffed it into her pocket.

Mr. Wingnutt, Dr. Clunk, and Mr. Quackenbottom had just finished jotting down their notes when Finley slipped back to her desk. The experts gave a final nod to Olivia and Henry, then looked at Finley expectantly.

Finley stood behind the LaughCrafter. This was her big chance. She could almost hear the joyful noise of laughter ringing out around the world. She pictured a new Glendale Elementary School swimming pool and imagined Mom and Dad driving the family to get pizza in their new lime-green convertible.

Finley cleared her throat. "Hello," she said. "My name is Finley Flowers, and this is my invention —

the LaughCrafter. It's a known fact that laughing makes you healthier by reducing stress. Studies show that people live longer if they laugh a lot. Laughter truly is the best medicine. And the LaughCrafter is designed to help people laugh more. So step right up, and try it today!"

Mr. Wingnutt, Dr. Clunk, and Mr. Quackenbottom inched forward.

Finley handed them each a sheet of paper. "The LaughCrafter has several special attachments," she explained. "These easy instructions will tell you how to use them."

As the experts read the instructions, Finley stepped back beside Henry, who had grabbed the salad fork from Olivia's model table setting and was using it to pry the Reusable Space Candy out of his mouth.

Dr. Clunk put on the reading glasses that hung from a silver chain around her neck. She picked up the joke book.

Finley held her breath as the experts flipped through the pages of Henry's hilarious jokes. No one laughed. Not even a smile. "Uh-oh," she whispered. "They don't get the jokes."

"Maybe dere waffing on dee inhide," said Henry, picking the last bits of Reusable Space Candy out of his teeth.

"Laughing on the inside doesn't count," said Finley.

Dr. Clunk put the joke book down and picked up her instruction sheet.

Mr. Quackenbottom pressed the laugh-track button, and Evie's goofy giggling bubbled out of the speakers. Mr. Quackenbottom winced. Mr. Wingnutt looked puzzled. Dr. Clunk scribbled notes.

"The canned laughs aren't working either," whispered Henry.

"It's okay," Finley said. "The funny-face-maker is up next. Who can resist a funny face?"

The visitors read the instructions, then clustered around the funny-face-maker. They studied it with furrowed brows.

Maybe they need new glasses, Finley thought.

"You have to get close," she told Mr. Wingnutt, "so you can see."

Mr. Wingnutt got close. He peered into the upside-down mixing bowl. Then he smoothed his hair and straightened his tie.

Olivia wrote in her notebook and showed it to Finley. It read: *funny faces = fail*, with a frown-y face.

Finley sighed. "I've still got my secret weapon," she whispered. "Plan D: the toe-tickler."

"I dunno," said Henry. "They don't look ticklish."

"Sometimes those are the most ticklish ones," said Finley.

Dr. Clunk read her instruction sheet and examined the toe-tickler. She took off her shoe, held her foot up to the forest of feathers, and gave the wheel a spin. The feathers swept along her sole as the wheel slowed. When it stopped, Dr. Clunk straightened her sock matter-of-factly and put her shoe back on.

Drat, thought Finley.

Mr. Wingnutt went next. As the feathers touched his toes, Finley thought she saw his top lip quiver. But it must have been a nervous twitch. He finished his turn, then made room for Mr. Quackenbottom.

Double drat, thought Finley.

Mr. Quackenbottom bent down and put the attachment to his foot.

Come on, Finley thought. *Just a little giggle.*

She held her breath . . . but there was no joyful noise.

Suddenly Mr. Quackenbottom stood up, a strange expression taking over his face. His brow crinkled. His eyes bulged. He looked as if he might explode.

"BWAAAAH-HUH-WAAAAAAAAH!" Mr. Quackenbottom burped the loudest, longest burp Finley had ever heard. It echoed across the room like a foghorn. Heads snapped to attention, and the whole class froze.

Dr. Clunk's eyebrows shot up. Mr. Wingnutt jumped back. Mr. Quackenbottom put his hand to his mouth as if to stop anything else from escaping.

"Nice one, Mr. Quackenbottom!" said Henry. "I guess The Burpolator worked!"

"Excuse me," Mr. Quackenbottom muttered sheepishly.

"Looks like Miss Manners worked, too," Olivia said, beaming. "That was *very* polite."

But suddenly, Olivia's smile vanished. "UUUUUUUUUUUUUURP!" she belched, louder than a lawnmower. "Excuse *me*," she whispered. Then her face turned as red as her "NO BURPING" sign.

A smile tugged at the corners of Dr. Clunk's lips. Mr. Wingnutt let out a chuckle. Mr. Quackenbottom snorted. Then they all burst out laughing.

Finley, Henry, and Olivia couldn't help it. They started laughing, too.

"Yay!" Finley cheered. "I knew the LaughCrafter would work — it just needed a little help!"

Turning around, she saw Lia and Kate giggling. The laughter spark had finally caught, and now it was spreading like wildfire down the line of desks!

Soon the whole class was filled with tee-hee-ing, hooting, and howling. Will was doubled over holding his stomach, and Henry had started his crazy seal noises. Everyone was cracking up, and the more they laughed . . . the more they laughed.

As Finley glanced around, she pictured happy flames of laughter racing through the city and across the state. She imagined them flowing down rivers and flying on airplanes, spreading warmth and light across the country and the world!

"I think you need to put a warning label on the LaughCrafter," Henry said between gasps. "Use with caution — laughter is contagious!"

"Ow-ow-ow!" Olivia cried. "My stomach hurts!" But she kept on laughing, wiping tears from her eyes. Then suddenly, she stopped. "Uh-oh," she whispered to Finley. "Here comes Principal Small."

Chapter 14

TEAM EFFORT

Finley spun around to see everyone looking in her direction. Principal Small was marching toward her, clip-clopping down the row of desks with Ms. Bird fluttering behind. She was a woman on a mission, and she was headed straight for Finley.

Finley's stomach lurched. She pictured Mom and Dad and Ms. Bird with their disappointed faces as Principal Small explained how Finley had disrupted the Invention Convention and was not a model fourth-grade citizen for Glendale Elementary School.

A lump grew in Finley's throat. *Maybe if I close my eyes and focus hard enough, I can sublimate myself,* she thought.

But when she opened them, Principal Small was standing right there. "Finley Flowers," she said like she was answering a question.

Finley smiled weakly. "Hello, Principal Small," she managed in her politest voice. "So nice to see you." She put out her hand and gave what she hoped was a firm-and-friendly handshake.

Principal Small pursed her lips together as she gestured to the LaughCrafter. "Is that what's responsible for this hullabaloo?"

Finley wasn't sure what hullabaloo was, but it didn't sound good. She glanced at Henry for help, but he was writing nervously in his notebook.

"Because it certainly livened up the Invention Convention," Principal Small continued. "I just wanted to see it for myself."

Finley breathed a sigh of relief. "Here it is," she said. "I call it the LaughCrafter. But it was really Henry's invention that made everyone laugh."

Henry grinned. "It was a team effort."

"Your inventions were both very creative," Ms. Bird chirped.

"Thanks," Finley and Henry said at once.

"What about mine?" Olivia piped up.

"Yours, too," said Ms. Bird. "Miss Manners saved the day." With that, she turned and walked Principal Small to the door.

"That reminds me," Olivia said to Henry. "You said you'd owe me for demonstrating The Burpolator. I think I did an excellent job."

"You did!" said Henry. "That was awesome!"

"So . . ." Olivia raised her eyebrows. "What do I get?"

Henry thought for a minute. "Unlimited lifetime use of The Burpolator. For *free!*"

Olivia shook her head. "No way. How about twenty bucks?"

"*Twenty bucks?*" Henry's eyebrows shot up.

Olivia shrugged. "That's a bargain. You said you'd owe me *big*, which means at least fifty, but I'll take twenty."

"Maybe you should wait," Finley suggested. "Someday you might need *his* help."

Olivia hesitated. "Fine," she said to Henry. "I guess it is kind of fun having you still owe me. Who knows when I might need something?"

Just then Ms. Bird rang the chime, and the class settled into silence. "It's time for our guests to go," she said, "but before they do, please join me in a round of applause to thank them for their time."

Everyone clapped. The special guests waved and smiled. Mr. Quackenbottom gave an awkward bow as they turned to go.

"I'll be passing out the feedback forms in a moment," Ms. Bird announced once the visitors had left, "but our guests wanted me to tell you they were very impressed."

Finley couldn't wait to read what the experts had to say about the LaughCrafter. They might have written a note offering to buy her idea! She held her breath as Ms. Bird darted around the room, calling out names: Will, Lia, Sam, Arpin, Kate . . .

"Finley Flowers!" Ms. Bird finally said, swooping in and sliding the feedback form onto Finley's desk.

Finley's heart pounded as she picked it up and read.

Henry leaned over in his seat. "So, what did they say?"

Finley finished reading, then set the paper down. "They said liked it," she said, frowning. "They really liked it."

Henry looked puzzled. "That's good, right? Why the sad face?"

"They *liked* it," Finley said. "But they didn't *love* it. And they didn't offer to buy my idea and sell it to the world."

Henry shrugged. "That doesn't mean you can't do it on your own."

Finley sighed. "I'm just a kid. I can't do anything on my own."

"Not true," said Henry. "You made the LaughCrafter. And look at Benjamin Franklin and all those other kid inventors. Besides, even if you had to wait till you were really old — like eighteen or even twenty — think of all of the other inventions you'd have by then!"

Finley groaned. "I'm not even ten yet. Twenty is a whole lifetime away!"

"Look, it just wasn't right for them," Henry said. "I mean, think about it — would you *really* want the LaughCrafter to be sold by the same company in charge of the collapsible toilet plunger or elephant-poo coffee filters?"

Finley tried to keep her frown down but couldn't. Henry always had a way of making her smile.

At recess, Finley and Henry headed for the swings. Finley pulled her sketchbook out of her pocket. "Ew," she said, peeking at the gummy goo that was sandwiched between the pages.

"I dunno about that Reusable Space Candy," Henry said with a shudder.

"I definitely won't be reusing it." Finley ripped out the sticky pages and threw them in the trash.

"But the LaughCrafter was great," Henry said, grabbing a swing.

"Thanks," said Finley, taking the next one over. "I can already think of one improvement, and the experts agreed."

"What?"

"A burp attachment," said Finley. "The Burpolator was definitely dazzling."

"Perfect!" said Henry. "The new and improved LaughCrafter Deluxe, now with built-in Burpolator! Or we could combine them — The BurpoLaughCrafter!"

"Sounds like a Hen-sational Fin-vention to me," said Finley. "I can't wait to try it out on Zack."

Finley leaned back and breathed in the cidery-sweet smell of fall. The wind whooshed through the branches above her, and a few orange and yellow leaves spiraled down. "Too bad I'm not going to make millions," she said. "I guess the LaughCrafter's not the next pet rock."

"Not yet," said Henry. "But bringing joy to the world is important. I think you should keep working on it. You make *me* laugh all the time."

Finley grinned. "You, too. A laugh machine is great. But nothing beats a Fin-tastic friend."

What's New?
Invention Starter

What You'll Need:

- Sheet of white or lined paper
- Pencil or pen

What to Do:

Get inspired: Come up with a problem or something people need or want. As you go about your day, notice all of the helpful devices we use all the time. And think of all of the problems people need help with. Sometimes ideas can sprout when you least expect it — like when you're talking to friends or playing.

Write down your ideas: Be ready to remember your ideas! Carry a pencil and notebook around so you can jot them down. You can even make your own pocket-sized idea journal.

Research: Do some research to find out more. Does anything like your idea already exist? If so, how can you make that same idea even better?

Name it: Think of a great name for your idea, something that sounds fun or interesting and lets people know what it is.

Draw it: Make a drawing or diagram of your invention. Don't forget to label the parts!

Write it: Write a description of your invention. Describe how you got your idea and what your invention does.

Build it: Make sure to have an adult supervise or help. Explain your invention and get permission to use your building materials to make a 3-D model of your invention.

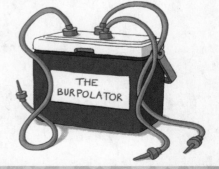

For Omi, who loved all kinds of art

TABLE OF CONTENTS

Chapter 1
FEELING FALL-ISH

Finley Flowers was running late. Mom had lost her keys again, and Finley's little sister, Evie, had taken forever to eat breakfast. When Mom dropped Finley and Evie off at school, Finley's best friend, Henry Lin, was waiting on the front steps.

"Earth to Finley! Hurry up!" Henry called as Evie skipped past him into the building.

Finley jumped for a leaf dangling from a branch and missed. "It's too nice to go inside! Fall's my favorite season — look, the trees are on fire!"

Henry glanced at his watch and made a beeline for the school doors. "We only have two minutes until class starts! Let's go!"

Finley and Henry got to their classroom just before the bell rang. Ms. Bird, their teacher, was waiting at the door. "Good morning, you two," she said in her chirpy morning voice. "You can unpack your things, but leave your jackets on — we'll be going right back outside."

"Woo-hoo!" Finley cheered. Fourth grade was the best! She might not get perfect grades like her older brother, Zack, but she loved school. Ms. Bird was always full of fun surprises.

Finley put away her books and peeked inside her lunchbox. Mom had packed a cucumber and cream cheese sandwich again. Evie's favorite — *not* Finley's.

Grrr, Finley thought. *I'm going to have to start making my own lunch.*

Once Ms. Bird had taken attendance, the class lined up at the door. Finley got a spot near the front. She could barely wait to find out where they were going. She was so hoppity, she felt like she was about to pop.

"What are we going to do?" Henry asked.

"We're going on a treasure hunt," Ms. Bird said with a mysterious look.

"Ahoy, me hearties!" Henry said in his best pirate accent. "We're off to search for treasure!"

Ms. Bird smiled. "Aye, Henry! Hopefully, we won't have to search too far."

Ms. Bird led the class outside and had them form a circle under a huge oak tree. "Today we're going to start a new unit of study," she explained. "We'll be looking at art, talking about art, and making art. On Monday we'll take our field trip downtown to the new art museum for some inspiration."

Finley lit up. *Finally!* she thought. She'd been waiting for the field trip for weeks. When Ms. Bird had passed out the permission slips, Finley had insisted that Mom sign hers right away.

The art museum was the perfect field trip for Finley. She'd considered being an inventor when she grew up, but being an artist was even better! After all, artists were kind of like inventors. They were always coming up with new things and being famous for making stuff. It was the ideal job for her — she had a million ideas, and she made stuff all the time!

"This morning, we'll warm up with an art activity," Ms. Bird continued. "Part one is a treasure hunt for fall leaves. Try to collect lots of interesting shapes and colors. You have ten minutes. Ready . . . go!"

Students scattered in all directions, darting from leaf to leaf like bees to flowers. Finley spotted a bright-yellow leaf and raced toward it. Olivia Snotham zoomed in and reached down to grab the same one, but Finley got there first.

"Aw!" Olivia pouted. "I wanted that one!"

"Here," Finley said, holding it out by the stem. "There are lots more."

"Thanks." Olivia took the leaf and held it up to the light.

Finley looked around, then plucked up a purple-ish-brown-ish one and a brilliant orange one. Her friends Kate and Lia ran past, scooping up handfuls of leaves and stuffing them into their pockets. A red maple leaf streaked by, and Finley lunged for it, colliding with Henry.

"Sorry!" they said together.

Henry laughed. "Whatcha got?"

Finley fanned out her leaves for him to see.

"Nice!" Henry said. "Look at this." He held out a yellow one tinged with rusty orange.

"Cool! Ooh, look — a lime-green one!" Finley said, pointing across the lawn. Then she dashed off to claim it for her collection.

Just as Finley had picked her tenth leaf, Ms.
Bird rang the chime. "Everyone line up!" she called.
"Bring your treasures with you — it's time for part
two!"

Finley squeezed in line behind Kate and Lia
and followed the rest of the students inside. When
they got back to the classroom, Ms. Bird opened
the cupboard and set some art supplies on the back
counter.

Finley couldn't wait to get started. She had never met an art material she didn't like. She liked the waxy, sweet smell of the crayons and the chalky softness of the pastels. She liked the silky-tipped watercolor brushes and the flat-bristled ones they used with thick tempera paint. Pencils, glue, clay, tissue paper — Finley loved them all!

Henry looked at Finley and grinned. "Turn on your Flower Power!" That was his nickname for the idea garden in her head where all her Fin-teresting thoughts grew.

Finley took her seat and arranged the leaves on her desk. There were three bumpy-edged oak leaves, two of the football-shaped purple-ish ones, three golden-brown ones with zig-zaggy edges, the lime-green one, and four so orange they looked like they'd glow in the dark.

Finley wondered what the assignment would be.

Who knows? she thought. *Maybe I'll make something so amazingly Fin-tastic they'll put it in a museum! This could be the start of something big!*

Chapter 2

WHIRLY, TWIRLY GIRL

Once everyone was seated, Ms. Bird walked up and down the rows, passing out sheets of big white paper and packs of colored pencils. "We're going to use the leaves we've collected to make leaf drawings," she explained. "Study them. Remember what the trees looked like, and try to capture the season of fall on paper."

Finley closed her eyes and pictured the falling leaves. She'd seen reds, greens, yellows, purples, and oranges. They'd made her feel whirly. Twirly. Fall-ish.

Maybe her drawing could make someone else feel fall-ish, too.

Ms. Bird put on some no-words music. "This piece by the composer Vivaldi is about fall," she said. "It might help get you in the mood."

As the violins started their stately melody, Finley picked up a bunch of colored pencils. The music swelled, and Finley moved her hand in big arcs and swirls, like leaves fluttering in the breeze. She imagined the wind blowing right through her pencils, coming out on her paper in wavy lines.

Finley was in the middle of a leaf whirlwind when Olivia stopped by her desk on her way to the pencil sharpener. Olivia looked at Finley's drawing and scrunched up her nose. "That doesn't look *anything* like fall," she said. "Fall is pretty."

Finley stopped drawing. Suddenly she didn't feel so fall-ish anymore. At camp last summer, she and Olivia had started to become friends, but sometimes

Olivia still said things in a not-so-nice way. Finley looked down at her paper and frowned.

"I just mean I've seen you draw better than that," Olivia added. "That looks like . . . scribbles."

Finley felt her cheeks turn red. "Well, they're *my* scribbles," she said. "And *I* like them."

Olivia shrugged and went to sharpen her pencils.

Finley studied her drawing again. *She* thought it was pretty. But pretty was in the eye of the beholder. She'd learned that last year when she bedazzled the mailbox. It had taken her hours to glue on all those jewels, and Mom and Dad hadn't appreciated her hard work.

It's just like Grandma always said, Finley thought. *You can't please everyone all the time.*

Finley decided to ignore Olivia and went right back to swirling. When she finished her drawing, she stepped back to get a better view.

Who cares about pretty anyway? she thought. *My art is interesting and fun!*

"All right, class," said Ms. Bird. "Time to line up for recess!"

As Finley pushed in her chair, Henry held up his drawing for her to see. In the middle of the paper was a small, lone leaf. It had been carefully outlined and colored in layers of red, orange, and gold. "I only had time for one," he explained.

"Wow!" Finley said. "It looks just like a real leaf!"

"Thanks," said Henry. "I tried to draw lots of details. Let's see yours."

Finley unrolled her drawing and held it up. Henry studied it with his hard-thinking face. "Um, no offense," he said, "but that does not look like a real leaf."

"It's not a leaf, exactly," Finley explained. "It's how a leaf *feels*."

Henry crinkled his forehead. "I don't get it," he said. "Leaves don't have feelings."

Finley laughed. "How do you know?" She put her drawing on Henry's desk and grabbed him by the arm. "Here," she said. "I'll show you."

They followed the rest of their classmates outside for recess, and Finley led Henry to the field by the playground. Then she took both of his hands in hers, leaned back, and spun around.

And around.

And around.

"This is how a leaf feels when it's blowing in the wind!" Finley shrieked. "All whirly and twirly!"

"Okay, okay!" Henry said, laughing. "Stop the ride! I get it!"

They tumbled onto the grass and watched the leaves spiral down.

"It's amazing how bright they are," Henry said, pointing. "They sure put on a show."

Finley grinned. *I'm going to put on a show, too!* she decided. *I'm going to be an artist and make my mark!*

Chapter 3
ART-SMART

Finley thought about the field trip all weekend. On Monday morning, she got up early and put on her artsy-est clothes: a red dress, yellow sweater, green tights, purple hairband, and sparkly blue shoes.

Perfect! she thought, checking her outfit in the mirror. *I look like a rainbow!*

Finley tucked her sketchbook and pencils into her backpack and bounded downstairs. Zack was already in the kitchen, sitting down to eat the last bagel.

"What's with the outfit?" he asked, shielding his eyes. "It's giving me a headache."

"Today's my class field trip to the art museum!" Finley announced. She grabbed some fruit salad out of the fridge and started arranging it into a colorful pattern on her plate. "We're getting inspiration for a special project."

Zack smeared more cream cheese on his bagel and took a big bite. "So?" he said, spraying crumbs as he spoke.

"*So*," said Finley, "it's exciting, and I'm dressing for the occasion. I make art all the time, but I've never seen real, famous art in person!"

"Your Popsicle-stick pyramids and tinfoil tiaras aren't exactly art," Zack said. He crammed the rest of his bagel into his mouth, grabbed his backpack, and headed to catch the bus. "I hope they let you in dressed like that. There might be a rule about not clashing with the exhibit."

Finley made a face behind Zack's back. Just because he was in sixth grade now, he thought he knew everything. Finley might not get straight As like he did, but she was art-smart — and this was her chance to shine!

When Finley turned around, Evie was sitting at the kitchen table. "Cool shoes," Evie said, pointing to Finley's feet. "Can I borrow them?"

"No."

Evie pouted. "Why not?"

"Because I'm wearing them," Finley said, pouring herself some cereal. "Besides, they wouldn't fit you."

"What about that hairband?" Evie asked, chomping on her toast.

Finley shook her head. "I'm using it right now. Maybe another time."

"Yes!" Evie clapped her hands together. "I'll wear it tomorrow with my new jeans! I love sharing!"

Finley sighed. *Of course you do*, she thought. *You're always the share-ee, and I'm the share-er.*

Sometimes Finley wished she could trade Evie in for a big sister instead — someone who'd have cool stuff *she* could borrow. But Mom and Dad would never go for that. Evie was seven, but she'd always be their baby. And Zack would always be the oldest — he got to do everything first, and he did everything perfectly. Finley was stuck in the middle of the sibling sandwich, and she was starting to feel squished.

Finley was finishing off her cereal when Mom swooped through the kitchen with her briefcase in one hand and her coffee in the other. Before Finley could remind her of the field trip, Mom had breezed out the back door. "In the car, girls!" she called over her shoulder. "Come on, or we'll be late!"

No! Finley thought. *Not today!* She grabbed her backpack and jacket and stopped to help Evie put her shoes on. Evie could do it herself — she just took forever, and she refused to wear Velcro.

Her little sister stuck out one foot and then the other, and Finley tied her laces. Then Evie bounded out the door.

"Thanks for being ready to go, big girl!" Mom said as Evie climbed into her booster seat.

Finley scowled. *It's not fair,* she thought. *I'm pretty much Evie's personal assistant, but she gets all the credit.* Finley looked down at her sparkly shoes. *And Mom didn't even notice my outfit.*

Lately, Finley wondered if anyone noticed her at all. Between all of Zack's sports practices and games and Evie's play dates, it didn't seem like there was much time left for her. But that was about to change.

Soon I'll be a famous artist, Finley thought. *Not just Finley-in-the-middle.*

Chapter 4
INVENTION #5

When Finley got to her classroom, she spotted Olivia sitting in the reading corner, doodling in a black sketchbook. She was dressed all in black — from her boots to the ribbon in her hair.

"You look . . . interesting," Olivia said as Finley headed for the bookshelves. "Why all the crazy colors?"

"I'm dressed for the art museum." Finley told her. "Why all the black? Are you trying to be a ninja?"

Olivia rolled her eyes. "No, *I'm* dressed for the art museum. Real artists wear black."

Finley looked down at her green tights and sparkly blue shoes. "How do *you* know what real artists wear?" she asked, frowning.

Just then Henry bounded over. "Whoa!" he said to Finley. "You look like a party!" He glanced at Olivia. "And *you* look like a ninja."

Ms. Bird walked to the front of the class and rang her chime. "Please sit down and clear your desks," she said. "The bus is waiting to take us on our museum adventure!" When everyone was seated, she took attendance, then started calling students to line up. Henry and Kate's row was first.

"I'll save you a seat," Henry whispered to Finley as he pushed in his chair.

Finley's row was last. Before Ms. Bird had finished calling her name, Finley sprang out of her chair to take her place in line. She checked her backpack for her sketchbook and pencils, then followed the class out the door.

As Finley boarded the bus, Henry waved her over. "Window seat?" he said, standing so she could squeeze in. "I tried to get one close to the front."

"Thanks." Finley plunked her bag down and slid the window open. She was already feeling bus-sick. Short trips were sometimes okay, but after about fifteen minutes on a bus, her stomach always felt like she was on a roller coaster.

"Hope it's not a bumpy ride," Olivia piped up from behind them. "Remember last year's field trip to the pumpkin patch? Someone had a little tummy trouble."

"Let's not bring it up," said Henry. "Get it — *bring it up*?"

"Yuck." Olivia wrinkled her nose. "I've never thrown up in my whole life. Mom says I have an extra-strong stomach."

Good for you, Finley thought, as she leaned her forehead against the cool window.

The ride to the art museum was loud and long. Henry read his *Weird and Wacky Bugs* book, and Olivia doodled in her sketchbook. Finley wished she could draw too, but even the idea of it made her stomach do backflips.

As they wove through downtown traffic, the skyscrapers got taller. Suddenly, the bus lurched to a stop in front of a massive stone building, and the doors opened with a wheeze. Students jostled down the aisle and spilled out onto the sidewalk.

Finley stepped into the fresh, crisp air. "Close one," she said, making a face.

"I could tell," said Henry. "You were getting as green as your tights."

"Ha." Finley turned to study the building. Part of it was modern and sleek, and part of it was like a castle, with turrets and tall, pointy-arched windows.

A real museum! she thought. *The place where art lives!* She felt better already. She could hardly wait to get inside.

The students followed Ms. Bird up the front steps of the museum, then filed through a set of heavy, glass doors into an entryway with giant columns.

"Wow," said Henry, looking up at the vaulted ceiling. "This place is huge."

Ms. Bird led them down a long hall. Chattering voices and squeaking shoes echoed off the marble-tiled walls.

Peering through an arched doorway, Finley noticed a canvas covered with splashes and streaks of paint. The colors looked like they were playing tag. They made her want to jump in and play, too.

I bet the artist had fun making that, thought Finley. *And now it's hanging in the museum. One day my art will be hanging here!*

The class turned down a smaller corridor and passed a row of landscape paintings in fancy gold and silver frames.

Finley could only dream of having her artwork displayed like that. Lately, there was barely enough room for *her* drawings on the fridge. They were always half-covered by Zack's soccer schedules and Evie's sticker-studded worksheets.

The class hurried on like a line of ants. Ms. Bird turned through an archway and stopped in an enormous room full of paintings. "Before we get started, I'm going to divide you into small groups so you can explore the gallery. When you're finished we'll move on to the next exhibit as a class."

Finley crossed her fingers. *Henry, Henry, Henry,* she thought.

Ms. Bird went around the room, splitting the students up into groups. Finally, she pointed to Finley, Henry, and Olivia. "You three," she said. "You're a group."

Yes! Finley thought. *It worked!*

Henry grinned and gave Finley a thumbs-up sign.

"Here's your first mission," Ms. Bird said to the class. "Observe the art and pick your group's favorite piece. Then take notes and do some sketches to help you remember what it looks like. There will be a homework assignment and a group art project based on what you see today. As part of the group project, which is due on Thursday," Ms. Bird continued, "you'll be answering a very big question: what is art?"

Finley looked around. *That'll be easy,* she thought. *Art is everywhere!*

"Okay, team," Henry said. "Let's go find a favorite!"

Finley, Henry, and Olivia toured the gallery. Henry read the plaques on the wall and carefully copied down names and dates. Henry loved lists.

Olivia stood in front of each piece of art, crossed her arms, and glared at it like she was having a staring contest. Then she opened her sketchbook, put

Claude Monet, 1840–1926

Alfred Sisley, 1839–1899

Berthe Morisot, 1841–1895

Pierre-Auguste Renoir, 1841–1919

Suzanne Valadon, 1865–1938

Edgar Degas, 1834–1917

Vincent van Gogh, 1853–1890

Mary Cassatt, 1844–1926

on her serious face, and took some serious notes.

Finley didn't believe in reading plaques or taking notes. She had her own way of observing. First she looked at the pieces from far away, then up close. She looked at them with one eye, then the other. She focused her eyes, then made them go blurry. She even leaned way over and looked at them upside down.

"What are you doing?" Henry asked, walking up behind her. "Yoga?"

"It's my special way of looking at art," Finley told him. "You should try it."

Henry bent forward, trying to copy her pose. "Ugh," he said. "It makes me dizzy."

At the far end of the gallery, Finley, Henry, and Olivia came to a painting of a girl sitting under an apple tree. As Finley studied the painting, she could almost feel the warm breeze and smell the fresh, grassy scent of summer. When she moved in close, the girl vanished and became rough patches of color. When she stepped back, the patches blended together, and the girl reappeared as if by magic.

"What about this one?" Henry suggested as he copied down facts from the plaque. "I like it the best. It looks so real. I feel like I could walk right into it."

"Those aren't exactly my colors," said Olivia. "There's no purple."

As they rounded the corner into the next room, Finley spotted the painting she'd noticed on the way in — the one with the playful splashes and streaks. "Those are *my* colors!" she said, pointing. "That's definitely my favorite."

Finley, Olivia, and Henry stood in front of the huge canvas. All the bright colors made Finley feel like dancing. She wished she could bottle up its squiggly lines and splooshy shapes and take them with her for when she was feeling droopy.

"It's called *Invention #5*," said Henry. "It reminds me of your whirly-twirly leaf picture."

"It doesn't look like anything." Olivia pointed across the room to a portrait of an important-looking man on a horse. The background was dark and dreary, and the man looked like he'd lost his hamster. "That's *real* art."

Real boring, thought Finley. *That belongs in a snooze-eum.*

"They both must be art," she told Olivia. "Or they wouldn't be in an *art* museum."

Finley turned back to *Invention #5*. When she studied the splatters and drips, it was almost like she was right there, watching the artist work.

It would be pretty cool to make your mark on the world by making marks, she thought. *Maybe if I look closely, I'll learn how.*

Chapter 5
FOOD FOR THOUGHT

Finley opened her sketchbook and started to draw. She looked up, then down, up, then down, trying to match her lines to what she saw. It was hard to copy the colors with a plain old pencil, but she tried to imagine them as different shades of gray.

As Finley put the finishing touches on her sketch, Ms. Bird strolled by and rang her chime softly. "Come with me, friends," she said. "Time for something completely different." She disappeared through a nearby doorway, and the class followed.

The next gallery was smaller than the first one, but every wall was covered with paintings of bowls of fruit and vases of flowers.

"Weird," Henry said, glancing around. "It's a room full of fruit."

Finley studied the piece next to her. It showed a blue-and-white ceramic bowl full of apples, peaches, pears, and grapes. Next to it, on a rumpled tablecloth, a cantaloupe was cut open, exposing its gooey insides. Hunks of cheese and bread were arranged on a cutting board, which sat beside a pitcher full of nodding sunflowers.

"Now I'm craving a snack!" said Henry. "Although that bread would be pretty stale. These paintings are hundreds of years old." He started copying names and dates into his notebook.

"I finally found *my* favorite," said Olivia, pointing to a painting of pink and purple flowers. "That would go perfectly in my room — it matches my bedspread."

Finley didn't care much about matching. Matching wasn't interesting. As she studied the piece next to her, she noticed something strange. In the middle of the food was a gold pocket watch. "That's funny," she said. "Someone forgot their watch."

"Hey," said Henry. "That painting has one, too. And the one over there has an hourglass."

"What's that?" Finley asked, pointing to the painting behind Olivia.

Olivia made a face. "Ew — a cockroach!"

"Actually, it's a beetle," Henry said, moving in closer to study it. "It looks real, but it's just painted."

"Yikes! Look at *that* painting!" Finley blurted out. "There's a skull — right in the middle of the food!"

Just then Ms. Bird rang her chime. "All right, class," she said. "Observe these still-life paintings carefully. What do you see?"

"Lunch?" Henry said with a hopeful grin.

Ms. Bird smiled. "Yes, fruits and cheeses and bread — and some other objects from daily life. What else?"

Olivia put up her hand. "Why does that one have a skull?"

"Maybe it's a *skull*-pture," Henry whispered to Finley. Finley giggled.

"Good question, Olivia." Ms. Bird pointed to the next painting over. "This one is also a still life. No skull here, but look." She pointed to the pocket watch lying in the folds of the tablecloth. "How is the watch similar to the skull? Or the half-burned candles in this one? Or the bubbles in that one? What do all of these objects tell us?"

"I don't know," said Olivia. "But it seems kind of useless to have a skull at a picnic. Not to mention gross."

"Why didn't the artist just put *living* people at the picnic?" Finley asked. "A skull can't even eat."

Ms. Bird nodded. "Unfortunately, it's too late for him — or her — to enjoy all that food. But it's not too late for us." She looked at Finley and raised her eyebrows. "Food for thought."

Suddenly Henry's stomach growled. "Sorry," he said. "I need some food for *eating*!"

Ms. Bird laughed. "Then let's go get some lunch. Follow me."

As the class funneled out the doors, they passed some writing on the wall that read, *"Ars longa, vita brevis. (Art is long, life is short.)"*

Finley wasn't sure exactly what that meant, or what those still-life paintings were about, but she did know they definitely weren't her style. When she made *her* marks, they'd be big and messy, like the splashes and splotches of *Invention #5*. They'd be bright and happy and impossible to ignore!

As the class filed down the corridor, Finley heard noises coming from a room to their right. Ms. Bird paused, then ushered them into a darkened theater where a video was playing. The man in the video was wearing big rubber boots and wading in a stream, breaking up branches and arranging them to form a giant nest that jutted out over the rushing water. In the next part of the video, he was standing in the middle of a green field, stacking rocks into a humungous egg-shaped tower. After that, he was kneeling on a beach beside the ocean, gluing icicles together with water to make a spiky, frozen star.

"What in the world is he doing?" whispered Olivia.

"Art?" Finley whispered back.

"I don't get it," said Henry. "What's the point?"

"Maybe he likes making things outside," Finley whispered. "Or maybe he's just having fun experimenting."

Ms. Bird gestured for the class to follow her and slipped out the back of the theater. "That art by Andy Goldsworthy was interesting," she said as they headed toward the museum café. "It was different from the other things we saw today — more like a whole art experience."

"I can't wait to experience the café," Henry said, fishing out his lunch money. "Those still-life paintings made me hungry."

Finley studied the menu as they waited in line. "I don't know what to get," she said. "The salads look good. But fall is soup season."

"You can't go wrong with cheese pizza," said Olivia.

Eventually Finley decided on potato soup and salad with a cranberry-oatmeal cookie for dessert. Henry ordered French toast with a side of French fries. "To go with all those French paintings," he explained.

Finley, Henry, and Olivia paid for their food and carried their trays to one of the marble-topped café tables. Henry drizzled syrup over his French toast and squirted his fries with ketchup. "So what's our favorite piece?" he asked.

"Definitely the vase of flowers," said Olivia, cutting her pizza into bite-sized pieces. "It was beautiful."

"I vote for *Invention #5* — the one with all the bright colors," said Finley. "I like that they're not

trying to be a person or place or thing. They're just being themselves."

"My favorite's still the portrait of the girl," said Henry. "She looked so real!"

"Well, *I'm* not going to change my mind," said Olivia. "I like what I like."

"We *all* like what we like," Finley said. "But we're supposed to pick *one* piece, not three."

"It looks like we have a problem," said Henry.

Finley frowned. "At least that's one thing we all agree on."

Chapter 6
GROUP WORK, SHMOOP WORK

On the bus ride back to school, Finley closed her eyes and thought about *Invention #5*. She imagined herself skipping across the canvas, joining the playful colors in their game of tag. Red had just tagged her on the arm, and she was running after Blue with a brush in one hand and a palette in the other. She swerved and cornered Green at the edge of the painting. Suddenly Green leaped right off the canvas onto the museum floor. Finley took a deep breath and jumped.

When she landed, Finley was standing outside a museum. A huge crowd stood nearby. Everyone was dressed in black. She was wearing black, too — a black beret and a long, black trench coat.

The important-looking man from Olivia's boring horse portrait strutted up in a black suit and introduced Finley. The audience exploded in applause. Then the man pulled a cord, releasing a giant, black sheet of fabric that hung across the front of the museum. It tumbled down like a waterfall, exposing humungous, sparkly, rainbow letters that read: *FLOWERS MUSEUM OF ART.*

As classical music filled the air, Finley tugged off the sash around her waist, and let her coat fall. Her dazzling, rainbow-sequined outfit sparkled in the sun.

The crowd went crazy, cheering and throwing flowers at her feet. Then they tore off their own jackets and coats to reveal a sea of beautiful, brilliant colors! Finley caught sight of Mom, Dad, Zack, Evie, and Olivia. Dad waved, looking proud, and Mom blew kisses and wiped happy tears from her eyes.

But wait a minute, Finley thought, *where's Henry?*

At that moment, over the chatter of the crowd and the symphony's serenade, Finley heard another noise — an engine! She looked up just in time to see a biplane zoom overhead, pulling a long banner that read: *FLOWER POWER*.

Henry saluted her from the cockpit. Finley waved up at him as he did a loop de loop, then circled back again.

Just then, Henry's voice echoed in her ear. "Earth to Finley! We're here."

Finley opened her eyes and glanced around. The museum and crowd were gone, and so was her sparkly outfit. She was sitting on a bus full of noisy kids. There was a crick in her neck, and she'd drooled on her shirt. She wasn't a world-famous artist with her very own museum — yet.

"I must have fallen asleep," she said dreamily.

"Yep," said Henry. "All that art wore you out."

When they'd gotten back to the classroom and put away their things, Ms. Bird rang the chime. "Grab a seat, everyone!" she said. "I hope you all enjoyed visiting the museum. I can't wait to hear your thoughts. For your group project, you'll be discussing your favorite museum piece and giving a presentation that answers the very big question I mentioned earlier."

On the board in humungous letters, Ms. Bird wrote:

WHAT IS ART?

"Does it have to be a *group* project?" Olivia piped up. "What if I have my own idea?"

Ms. Bird smiled. "Then share it with your group! You have half an hour to brainstorm, so go ahead and get started."

Group work, shmoop work, Finley thought. But she grabbed her sketchbook and pulled a chair up to Olivia's desk.

"You go first," Henry told Olivia, "since you already have an idea."

Olivia sighed. "Fine. But you're not going to like it." She cleared her throat. "Art is beautiful. So we'll paint a beautiful still life with flowers and play some beautiful music to go with it." She looked at Finley and Henry expectantly.

"Hmm," said Henry.

"That's it?" said Finley.

"See?" said Olivia. "I knew you wouldn't like it."

"It's just that I don't think that answers the very big question," Henry said. "Because not all art is beautiful."

Olivia frowned. "Do you have a better idea?"

Henry made his thinking-hard face. "We could do portraits and talk about how art freezes a moment in time, like that painting of the girl under the tree."

"But what about *my* painting — *Invention #5*?" said Finley. "It showed the parts of art — lines and shapes and colors."

Olivia shook her head. "I *still* don't get why you like that one."

Just then, Ms. Bird came to check in on the group. "How's the brainstorming going?"

"Not so good," said Olivia. "They don't like my idea."

Finley shrugged. "Well, you don't like ours either."

"It's not that we don't like it," Henry told Olivia. "We just have our own ideas."

"Maybe we could divide up our twenty-five minutes and do three separate presentations," Finley suggested. "That way we could all do what we want. Problem solved!"

"Now, *that's* a good idea," said Olivia. "We'd have eight minutes and twenty seconds each."

Ms. Bird shook her head. "I'm afraid that won't work. That would be three individual projects. For a group art project, you have to work *together*."

Olivia sighed. "I guess we're stuck then."

"I guess so," said Finley.

* * *

Finley's group spent the rest of the afternoon brainstorming, but they still couldn't settle on an idea for their project.

"Maybe we can work on it after school tomorrow," Henry suggested. "I don't have soccer practice."

"Sure," Finley said. "We can meet at my house if you want."

Just before it was time to pack up for the day, Ms. Bird rang the chime. "Class, before we go, I want to explain today's homework — it's an art assignment, due tomorrow."

Finley turned her chair around and put on her listening ears.

"Sometimes artists use observation," Ms. Bird continued. "They look carefully at the world around them, like in the still-life paintings at the museum. Your homework for tonight is a fall harvest still life. Arrange some foods from your fridge and sketch them. After that, write a short poem to go with your drawing."

Suddenly, fireworks went off in Finley's head. *This could be my chance!* she thought. *I'll make something Fin-tastic, and everyone will love it. Then Henry and Olivia will listen to me!*

Chapter 7
MOLDY MASTERPIECE

When Finley got home from school, she cleared off the dining room table. She was already picturing her class gathering around to congratulate her on the still life and tell her what a great artist she was. She'd make a big splash and get Olivia and Henry to see her point of view at the same time. Mom and Dad would definitely reserve a spot on the fridge for her after that!

Finley got her craft box and took out some pencils and a piece of drawing paper. It was time to put her plan into action. "Hey, Mom," she called, "do we have a tablecloth? Maybe a lacy one that looks expensive and old?"

Mom was drifting from one room to the next, looking for her wallet. "I don't think so, honey," she said, poking her head through the doorway. "What's it for?"

"My fall still life. I want it to look fancy, like the ones we saw in the museum today."

"Could you use something else?" Mom asked. "Like a dishtowel?"

Finley frowned. "A dishtowel is *not* fancy."

Just then, Mom spotted her wallet in the basket of found things on the kitchen counter. "You'll have to look around, sweetie," she said, grabbing the wallet. "I've got to run — I'm late for book club." She kissed Finley's forehead and slung her bag over her shoulder. "Maybe Dad can help."

Finley sighed. If anyone was going to help her find something fancy, Dad was not that person. "What about fruits and veggies?" she asked. "Do we have anything colorful?"

Mom headed for the door. "Look in the fridge," she said over her shoulder. "There's not much, but I'm going shopping tomorrow."

Drat, thought Finley. *Tomorrow is too late. If it were Zack's homework, I bet she'd drop everything and go shopping today.*

Finley rummaged through the kitchen drawers. She found balls of rubber bands, chip clips, coupons, chopsticks, birthday candles, and millions of twist ties, but nothing that even resembled a lacy tablecloth.

Just then, Finley had a brilliant brainstorm — she could use Dad's paisley bathrobe! She grabbed it from the hook in his closet and spread it out across the dining room table so it looked artfully messy, like someone had just happened to throw it down.

Now for the fruits and veggies, Finley thought. She opened the fridge and peered inside. There was nothing fresh and colorful like in the still-life paintings at the museum. Just smelly, shriveled-up mushrooms, a couple of scraggly carrots, a bruised apple, some withered lettuce, and half of a sad-looking onion wrapped in plastic. They were all dingy and dull. And they didn't smell so great either.

Finley was about to give up when she unearthed a hunk of orange cheddar that had been hiding behind the hummus. It was crumbly and half-covered in blue-green mold. *At least it's got some color*, she thought.

Next she grabbed a couple of slices of bread and an almost-empty bottle of juice. She arranged everything on the bathrobe next to the crispy remains of Mom's African violet.

"Voilà," Finley muttered. *"Wilted Still Life with Dead Plant." It might not be pretty*, she thought. *But it's still. And it's life.*

At that moment, Evie bounded into the room. "Ooh!" she said, holding her nose. "What are you *doing?*"

"It's called a still life," said Finley. "It's for school."

"It looks pretty dead to me," said Evie. "Maybe it's a *zombie* still life!"

"Out!" said Finley, pointing to the door.

"*Okay.*" Evie scurried backward into the kitchen. "But don't say I didn't warn you . . ."

Finley walked around the table, surveying her still life from all angles. Something was missing, but she couldn't figure out what. Finally she gave up, grabbed her colored pencils, and took a seat. *All right*, she thought. *Time for some Fin-spiration.*

Finley sketched and shaded. She striped and swirled. Just as she was adding rainbow-colored rings to the onion, Zack came in and plunked his backpack down beside her.

"What is *that*?" he said, eyeing the strange arrangement.

"My homework." Finley said, coloring the bruise on the apple a brilliant blue. "It's a fall still life."

"Wow," Zack said. "That's one funky fall still life."

Finley glared at her brother. "Don't *you* have homework to do or something? Maybe a test to study for?"

"I was going to get a snack first," Zack said. "But I just lost my appetite."

Zack tromped upstairs, and Finley put down her pencil. *The problem with this fall still life is that there's nothing fall-ish about it*, she realized.

Suddenly, Finley had an idea. She dashed to the backyard and collected the best leaves she could find. Then she marched back to the dining room and stuck them between the other objects in her still life. *There*, she thought. *That adds some fall flavor!*

Finley had just finished drawing the leaves and was working on shading the neon-green mold on the cheese when Dad came out of the office.

"What is that smell?" he called from the kitchen.

"My still life!" Finley answered. "It stinks!"

"Come on," Dad said, poking his head through the dining room doorway. "It can't be that bad."

"No," Finley said. "I mean it actually smells."

Dad came a little closer. "Oh," he said, sniffing. "You're right. Don't we have anything you can draw that's less . . . ripe?"

"Nope," said Finley, shaking her head. "I'm making the best of what I've got."

"Well, I guess it shows nature in action," Dad said. "That's what happens when you leave things too long. You've got to eat them while you can. Seize the day, I always say!" He picked up the phone. "I'm going to order a pizza for dinner."

Seize the day! Finley's heart leaped. That gave her a great idea! She ran to her room and grabbed the glow-in-the-dark watch she'd gotten for her birthday. Then she stretched it out on the table so it dangled off the edge, just like the pocket watch in the still life at the museum.

Finley added the watch to her drawing, making sure to include the time — 5:21 p.m. Then she stood back to take a look. It was a still life, but it didn't look still. Colors zoomed and zipped across the paper! Lines wiggled and waved!

Fin-tastic! Finley thought. *This still life is sure to make a splash!*

Chapter 8
SEIZE THE CHEESE

After lunch the next day, Finley hurried back to her classroom. She took one last look at her drawing and practiced reading the poem she'd written the night before. This was her chance to shine, and she wanted to be ready.

Finally, Ms. Bird stood at the front of the room and rang the chime. "All right," she said, "it's time to share your homework." She glanced around the class. "Who would like to go first?"

Before Finley could raise her hand, Olivia's arm shot into the air. Ms. Bird nodded in her direction. "Olivia?"

Olivia walked to the front, unfolded a big, wooden easel, and draped some wispy fabric over it for decoration. When she set her drawing on the easel, a murmur went through the room. Delicately shaded fruits and vegetables rested on a flowery tablecloth, along with forks, patterned plates, and a pair of silver goblets. The apples, grapes, and pears were plump and round; the eggplants and peppers were smooth and shiny; the bread and cheese were broken into beautiful, artistic hunks.

Sheesh, Finley thought, *the inside of Olivia's fridge must look like a royal picnic.*

"This is my still life," Olivia announced, "inspired by the paintings at the museum. I tried to show the beauty of the fall harvest. My poem is entitled 'Feast':

Fancy forks and pretty plates —

A table set for two.

Pink and purple flowers

In a vase that's white and blue.

Yummy fruits and veggies

Are a feast for eyes to see —

A still life to remind us

Of how sweet life can be."

Olivia smiled primly as she finished.

Oh, for crying out sideways, Finley thought. *She doesn't even like fruits and veggies!*

"Thank you," said Ms. Bird. "That was just lovely."

The class clapped, and Olivia curtsied. She grabbed her drawing, folded up her fabric and easel, and sashayed back to her seat.

Finley hesitated. Now that she'd seen Olivia's still life, she wondered if hers would make a splash after all. She took a peek at her artwork's swirly, brilliant colors.

It's different, Finley told herself. *It's special.*

She decided to wait and go last. That way, she'd make a lasting impression.

Henry volunteered to go next. He'd drawn a still life of take-out containers. Some were stacked into towers, and others were lying on their sides with food spilling out.

"Are those spring rolls?" Will blurted out. "I love spring rolls!"

Henry nodded. "We had Thai food last night. My poem is a haiku. I called it 'Dinnertime' because that's what it's about.

Steaming boxes hold
Gifts of curry and noodles.
Please pass the soy sauce."

The class clapped as Henry finished. His cheeks turned pink as he rolled up his drawing and took his seat.

"Henry, your still life was so realistic," said Ms. Bird. "I think you've made us all hungry!"

One by one, the students showed their art and read their poems. When everyone else had finished, Finley marched to the front of the class and unfurled her drawing.

"Finley," said Ms. Bird, "can you tell us about your piece?"

"Well . . ." Finley paused and took a deep breath. "I gathered some things from the fridge and arranged them. Then I drew what I saw. I was worried because the still-life paintings at the museum looked fancy, and we didn't have anything fancy in our fridge. In fact, that right there is some *really* moldy cheese."

Finley glanced at Olivia, who made a face like she'd just taken a bite of it.

"But then I remembered that art isn't always beautiful," Finley continued. "So this is our dining room table on October 14 at 5:21 p.m. I put in the watch to show that time is passing, just like the paintings at the museum. I also added some color to make things more interesting and some leaves to make it more fall-ish."

Finley set the drawing down on Ms. Bird's desk and took out her sketchbook to read what she'd written. "My poem is called 'Seize the Cheese':

Life is short, so seize the cheese!
Be happy that you're in it.
Make the most of every day —
Don't miss a single minute.
Just like all this funky food,
I wouldn't want to waste it.
(I'm glad I made it into art
So I don't have to taste it!)"

When Finley was finished, Ms. Bird smiled. "Thank you, Finley. You didn't draw it *exactly* the way you saw it, but it was very interesting — and inspiring! I might have to go home and clean out my fridge tonight."

There was a trickle of applause and a wave of whispers as Finley took her seat. "So," she said to Henry, "what did you think of my still life?"

"It was a *moldy*, but a goodie," Henry said. "Get it?"

Finley didn't laugh. She could tell that Henry didn't really get her drawing. And neither did anyone else. *So much for my chance to shine*, she thought.

"Class, thank you for sharing your wonderful still-life artwork," Ms. Bird said. "You can take a ten-minute rest break, and then we'll move on to science."

As soon as Ms. Bird had finished, everyone crowded around Olivia and Henry to get a closer look at their drawings.

"Those spring rolls look so real!" Kate said to Henry.

"Yours belongs in the museum!" Lia told Olivia. "I bet you'll be famous one day!"

Finley stared at her moldy cheese and held back her tears. *The cheese stands alone*, she thought glumly. *I'll never be an artist. I'll never be the one people notice.*

Chapter 9
A VERY BIG IDEA

After the dismissal bell rang, Finley quietly gathered her things and slipped out the door. She didn't tell Ms. Bird to have a Fin-tastic night. She didn't wait for Henry so they could walk home together. She didn't notice the sunshine or the way-up-high clouds. And she didn't hear the leaves as they crunched under her feet.

When Finley got home, there was a big bowl of apples on the kitchen counter. Someone had gone shopping.

It figures, Finley thought, staring at the mound of fresh, glossy fruit.

Just then Zack bounded in through the back door with his soccer stuff on. "How'd it go with the stinky still life?" he asked, snatching an apple from the bowl.

"I don't want to talk about it," Finley muttered unhappily.

Zack shrugged. "Suit yourself."

Finley grabbed her backpack and slunk up to her room. She closed the door and flopped onto her bed. Then she took out her sketchbook and flipped to her drawing from the field trip. Her *Invention #5* didn't look anything like the painting in the museum.

It's no use, Finley thought. *I'll never be famous.* She glared at the sketch. Then she crumpled it up, aimed for the trash can, and missed.

Just then, there was a knock at the door.

"Anybody home?" Henry asked, opening it a crack and peering in.

"What are *you* doing here?" Finley asked.

"Looking for you. Your brother said to come on up." Henry scooped up the crumpled ball of paper and slam-dunked it into the trash. "Two points!"

Finley groaned.

"Where have you been?" Henry asked. "What's wrong?"

"What's wrong is that I want to be a famous artist, but no one appreciates my style," Finley said. "I should forget it and copy someone else's."

"No way," Henry said. "All those pieces we saw in the museum weren't there because they looked like someone else's. Artists do their own thing, even if other people don't always like it."

Finley sighed and looked away. "That's easy for you to say — everyone *loved* your still life. Olivia's, too."

"Speaking of Olivia, she's waiting downstairs," Henry said. "We were supposed to come over and work on our group project after school, remember?"

Finley shook her head. "You and Miss Perfect should just do the project without me. It'll be better that way."

Henry frowned. "Weren't *you* the one who said art is *fun*?"

Finley looked at Henry, and a tear slid down her cheek.

"Come on," Henry said. "It's a group project, and it's due in two days. We need you."

Finley sniffed and grabbed a tissue from the box by her bed. "We're never going to answer the very big question. We can't even agree on anything small."

Henry walked to the door. "Well, Olivia and I are here, so we might as well try."

Finley picked up her sketchbook and followed Henry downstairs. Olivia was waiting in the kitchen, where Evie was practicing her magic show.

"Hey," Evie said, "want to see some tricks?"

"Maybe later," said Finley. "Why don't you try them out on Mom first?"

"Okay," Evie said. She flung her cape over her shoulder and waved her wand in the air. "Close your eyes, and I'll disappear!"

Is that all I have to do? Finley thought. She closed her eyes and heard Evie dash into the living room. When she opened them, Olivia and Henry were looking at her.

"Where did *you* disappear to after school?" Olivia asked.

"Sorry," Finley said, taking a seat at the kitchen table. "I forgot we were meeting. I was too busy thinking about my failure of a still life."

"It was kind of . . . different," Olivia admitted. "But I wouldn't call it a *failure*."

Finley frowned. "It definitely wasn't a success."

Olivia looked at Henry. Henry looked at Finley. Finley looked out the window.

"Why don't we go outside?" Henry suggested. "Maybe the fresh air will help us get some fresh ideas."

Finley searched through the cupboards and grabbed some granola bars. Then they headed to the backyard.

"I want to sit in the hammock," said Olivia.

"Come on," Finley said. "There's room for three."

Finley, Henry, and Olivia all piled onto the hammock and leaned back to watch the clouds.

What is art? Finley wondered. The very big question was harder to answer than she'd thought.

"I wish we could do something really different," Finley said.

"Why can't we just use my idea?" Olivia whined. "That would be easy."

"Easy for *you*," said Henry.

Olivia rolled her eyes.

"Maybe in order to answer the very big question," said Finley, "we need a very big idea." She twined her fingers around the silky hammock rope.

"We could take the whole class on a very big field trip," Olivia suggested. "I've always wanted to go to Paris. *That* would be fun!"

"Sounds good to me," said Henry. "Just think of all that yummy food!"

"*Or* we could combine all our ideas into one," Finley said. "Something beautiful that captures a moment. Something different and *fun* . . ."

Just then the breeze blew, showering them with leaves. "Look what we caught," Henry said, picking some out of the hammock. "Little pieces of fall!"

Another gust sent a leaf sailing right into Finley's lap. "Hey," she said, twirling it by the stem. "I think I've got it!"

"What?" asked Olivia.

Finley's eyes widened. "A totally art-rageous idea!"

Chapter 10
UNBE-LEAF-ABLE

Finley, Henry, and Olivia didn't have much time to plan. But they divided up the work, and by Thursday, they were ready to present their project. That morning, Finley met Henry and Olivia in front of the school. "It's a great day to make some art!" she said. "Are you ready?"

Henry grinned. "Let's do this!"

Olivia patted her backpack. "I've got the fabric and yarn in here. And that magic wand and cape your sister lent us will be perfect!"

They stood on the school steps and looked out on the lawn. "That's going to be the best spot for our project," said Henry.

"Yep," said Olivia. "Right where everyone will see it."

When they got to the classroom, Ms. Bird greeted them at the door. "Go ahead and unpack your bags and take your seats," she said. "We're going to start the day with our presentations. That way we'll be done in time for recess."

"I think we should save ours for last," Olivia said to Finley and Henry. They both nodded in agreement.

Finley tried to pay attention as the other students shared their projects, but she was extra hoppity. Amelia, Frances, and Arpin recreated an ancient Greek mosaic they'd seen on the field trip. Kate, Lia, and Will demonstrated ten different art materials and made a landscape like their favorite one from the museum. Harper's group shared a book they'd made about the artist Mary Cassatt.

Finally, it was Finley's group's turn.

"All right, class," said Ms. Bird, "we have one more presentation — Finley, Henry, and Olivia."

Olivia turned off the lights and stood at the front of the class. Henry went to the back of the room and put on the cape. Then Olivia pressed a button on the remote control and a picture of a humungous flower painting came up on the white board.

"Some people might think that pretty isn't important," Olivia began, "but looking at pretty scenes and objects can make you feel good. Art can remind everyone that the world is beautiful. It can even make a tiny flower into a big deal. Isn't that an awesome blossom?"

Henry gave Finley a nod, and she put on some mysterious music. Then Henry walked down the center aisle waving Evie's magic wand. When he got to the front, he spun around. "Art is magical!" he said in a low voice. "It can take us back to a moment in history."

Olivia pressed the remote, and a slide of a still life came up on the board.

"Does this look familiar?" Henry asked. "It's a still life from hundreds of years ago, just like the ones we saw in the museum. Art captures a moment in time. Like Finley pointed out in her poem, it reminds us to 'seize the cheese' before it gets moldy. Remember how those still-life paintings included all that weird stuff? Bubbles pop, candles melt, minutes tick away on watches, and flowers fade. Time passes, but art keeps things, places, and people alive."

Finley turned on the lights. "Art isn't just about the artist or the subject," she said. "It's about the people looking at it, too. Our project involves participation — so follow me!"

Ms. Bird and the rest of the class followed Finley, Henry, and Olivia out to the front of the school.

"Today we're going to make some art outside," Finley explained. "And everyone is going to help! Don't worry, we'll show you how. First, find a partner. Then come get some of Olivia's netting and two pieces of yarn." Finley reached into Olivia's bag and pulled out some see-through fabric and yarn.

"Tie a piece of yarn around each end of the fabric, like this," Henry said, knotting the yarn and pulling it tight.

"Next, pick a pair of trees and stretch the fabric between them," Finley said as she and Henry demonstrated. "Make sure they're close enough for the fabric to hang down like a net. Then tie the yarn around each tree trunk to make a leaf hammock!"

Finley and Henry finished tying their hammock and stepped back. "The hammocks will catch the leaves as they fall from the trees," Finley explained.

"You can even gather some leaves off the ground and fill yours partway to give it a head start."

"But don't get in it!" Henry warned. "It's a *leaf* hammock, not a people hammock."

Students formed a line in front of Olivia to get their fabric, then wandered around the yard, picking out pairs of trees. They tied their hammocks high and low, near and far. Soon there were twelve of them, hanging like wispy cocoons in front of the school.

Olivia glanced around. "It's working!" she said to Finley. "They're beautiful!"

Henry grinned. "They're unbe-*leaf*-able!"

Suddenly, the wind blew, and a flurry of leaves fluttered down.

"We caught some!" Lia shouted, pointing to the leaves suspended in her netting.

"We did, too!" yelled Will.

Everyone started scooping up leaves. Soon the hammocks were bulging, suspended like giant seedpods all over the lawn.

"Look!" Finley said to Henry and Olivia. "A whole herd of hammocks!"

"Hooray for hammocks!" Henry said, grabbing a handful of leaves and tossing them in the air.

Before long, someone started a game of freeze tag, and Lia and Kate got into a leaf fight with Will and Arpin.

"Class!" Ms. Bird called. "I know it's hard to stop, but we need to get to recess. Let's gather around so Finley, Henry, and Olivia can finish up."

Finley, Henry, and Olivia stood behind their hammock. "In closing," said Henry, "we just wanted to say that art is . . . art! It can make you pay attention to things and help you remember a moment, person, or place."

"It can be beautiful," said Olivia. "Or it can just *be*."

"There are so many different types of art and so many reasons people make it," said Henry. "We made a list, and it filled up five pages of my notebook!" He held up his notebook and flipped through the pages to prove it.

"At first we couldn't agree on what to do for our presentation," said Olivia. "We were brainstorming in Finley's hammock when she got the idea. It was inspired by a falling leaf and by that video we saw at the museum of that man who made art out of nature."

"It was Olivia's idea to sit in the hammock in the first place," said Finley. "She also thought of using the fabric. And Henry figured out how to hang it."

"Thanks for helping create our leaf hammocks!" said Henry.

"We made something beautiful *and* captured a moment in time *and* had fun doing it," said Finley. "We hope you had fun, too!"

"I like how this group project turned into a class project!" said Ms. Bird. "Let's get a class picture! Everybody squeeze in together. On the count of three . . ."

Finley glanced over at Henry and Olivia. "Ready?" she whispered, grasping the edge of the hammock.

"One . . ." Ms. Bird held the camera up. "Two . . . three!"

Finley, Henry, and Olivia shook the hammock, and leaves flew everywhere. They drifted down like confetti as the class clapped.

Ms. Bird snapped the picture. "Gotcha! Well done, everyone. That was quite the *Fin*-ale."

Chapter 11
TASTES LIKE FALL

That night at dinner, Evie plunked her plate down next to Finley's. "I saw your leaf hammocks in front of the school!" she said, helping herself to chips and salsa. "They were waving around like ghosts in the wind! I told Lucas they were tree spirits, and he got scared and told Mr. Green."

"*I* spotted them after soccer practice," Zack said. "You could see them from halfway down the block. They looked pretty awesome."

"That's our creative girl," Dad said, smiling proudly. "Always thinking up something interesting."

"*Fin*-teresting," Mom corrected.

Wow, Finley thought. *Maybe they do notice me after all.* "Thanks," she said. "We had fun making them — the whole class helped. And Ms. Bird told us that Principal Small is going to hang a picture of them in the hallway so people can still see our project after we take the hammocks down. She wanted to remind everyone that we can do big things when we work together. And she's going to throw us an art party tomorrow afternoon!"

"Lucky!" said Evie. "You get to do all the good stuff! All *we* do is coloring, and Mr. Green says you have to stay in the lines."

"Maybe we can make some leaf hammocks in the yard," Mom suggested. "Finley could show us how."

"Sure," Finley said. "I can ask Olivia where she got the fabric."

Zack nodded. "That'd be cool."

Suddenly Evie's eyes grew wide. "We could fill them with candy!" she shrieked. "Or put mummies in them for Halloween!"

Dad laughed. "Haunted hammocks! We'll have the best-decorated house in the neighborhood. We could even start a Halloween tradition."

"*This* mummy wouldn't mind an after-dinner rest," Mom said when they'd finished eating. "Anyone up for watching the sunset? It's so pretty out."

"Can we bring dessert?" Evie asked as Finley and Zack helped clear the table.

Mom smiled. "Why not?"

Dad cut up some slices of freshly baked pumpkin bread and grabbed a stack of plates and napkins. Then everyone followed him to the backyard. They crunched through the sea of leaves and headed for the hammock.

"Pretty soon it'll be raking time," Dad said.

Zack groaned. "Don't remind me."

"Up you go," Mom said, holding the hammock still so Evie could climb in.

Finley flopped down beside Evie, and Zack sat beside Finley. The sun was just sinking below the trees, casting a pinkish-orange glow on their faces and on the rows of feathery clouds that streaked the sky.

"Thanks for letting us use your cape and wand," Finley said to Evie. "They worked great for our presentation."

Evie stopped wiggling her loose tooth and grinned. "No problem. You let me borrow your stuff all the time."

Zack rested his foot on the ground and rocked the hammock gently. Finley leaned her head back and closed her eyes. She could hear the humming and honking of far-away traffic. There was a chill in the air, but with Zack and Evie on either side of her, she was warm. At that moment, being Finley-in-the-middle didn't feel so bad. In fact, it felt like she was right where she belonged.

"Here you go," Dad said, handing them each a plate of pumpkin bread. "It's a new recipe. Hope you like it."

Evie took a big bite. "I love it," she mumbled. "It tastes like cinnamon."

Finley broke off a piece and popped it into her mouth. It was still warm, and spicy-sweet. *"Mmm,"* she said. "It tastes like fall."

Chapter 12
P-ART-Y!

The next day after lunch, Finley, Henry, and Olivia raced back to their classroom. All the desks had been pushed together into groups and covered with thick brown paper. Music was playing, and Ms. Bird's desk was draped with a checked tablecloth. Fruits, cheeses, and crackers were artfully arranged next to a pitcher of punch and stacks of paper plates and napkins.

"Woo-hoo!" Henry hollered. "Let's get this p-*art*-y started!"

Ms. Bird laughed. "All right," she said. "But first let me go over the activities." She paused as the class gathered around. "We have a drawing station with colored pencils and markers; a collage station with magazines and paper to cut and paste; a sculpture station with recycled plastic and cardboard, and masking tape and wire for building; and a painting station where you can mix your own colors and make your mark on the class canvas." She pointed to the back counter, where a huge piece of painting canvas had been unrolled and taped in place. "Choose your favorite activity, or try them all. There's also a snack station with an edible still life on my desk, so please help yourselves."

"Cool!" said Henry. "We can finally eat the still life!"

Ms. Bird smiled. "Let me know if you need any help," she said. "And don't forget the most important part — have fun!"

Finley, Henry, and Olivia went straight to the painting station. Finley got a big brush and squeezed some red and yellow paint onto her palette. She mixed them together, then added the tiniest bit of black. "Look," she said. "I made up my own color. I call it Fiery Fall."

Henry peered over Finley's shoulder. "I call it orange."

"It's a certain *type* of orange," said Finley. "My special color recipe."

Henry helped himself to yellow and blue. "My color's going to be Mantis Green," he said, "after my favorite bug."

"I want to mix my own signature color, too," said Olivia, reaching for the blue and red.

"Let me guess," said Henry, "Princess Purple?"

"No," said Olivia. "Perfect Plum."

Once Olivia had finished mixing, they took their palettes and brushes over to the big canvas. They made wavy lines and squiggles and dots.

"I have to admit, that does look pretty cool," said Olivia, "even though it's just colors."

Finley glanced around the room. Everywhere she looked, students were making stuff. Lia was building a castle out of toilet paper rolls and plastic bottles. Kate was cutting up magazines to make a collage. Will was working on a feathery sculpture that looked like a giant cat toy.

"What should we do now?" Finley asked.

"What about portraits?" Henry suggested, pointing to the drawing station.

"All right," said Olivia. "But let's make them good."

Finley and Henry got the clipboards, and Olivia passed them some paper. "We should try to show who we *really* are, not just the way we look," said Finley. "Like that painting of the girl at the museum."

Henry grabbed a pencil. "I'll do your portrait," he told Finley.

"I'll draw you," Finley told Olivia, "as long as you're not mad if it's not the most beautiful portrait."

"You can do it however you want," said Olivia. "Just try to include my new barrettes."

Finley grinned. "Deal."

"I'll do yours then," Olivia said to Henry.

"Prepare to be portrait-ed!" Henry announced. "Ready . . . set . . . draw!"

Finley studied Olivia's face. It was like she was seeing her for the first time — her wide, blue eyes, her silky bangs, the way the right corner of her mouth turned down just slightly when she was concentrating. Finley's marker danced across the page.

"Hold still!" said Henry. "You're drawing with your whole body!"

"I'm a person," Finley told him, "not a still life! I can't sit as still as an apple." She drew Olivia with swirly eyes, pink cheeks, curly hair, and rainbows coming out of her ears to show how she was always thinking. Then she added a wispy-fabric scarf and purple curls in Olivia's hair to match her barrettes.

"It's Fin-ished!" Finley announced, holding up her drawing.

"Whoa, that was fast!" said Henry. "It's really . . . colorful."

Finley nodded. "I tried to show her spunk."

"I have spunk?" Olivia asked.

"You've been spunk-ified!" said Henry.

Olivia examined the drawing. "It's not exactly my style," she said. "But it is pretty cool. Let's see yours, Henry."

Henry hesitated. "I'm still working on it — it's hard to capture the essence of Finley, especially when she won't hold still."

Finley tried not to move a muscle. But suddenly she had itches all over, screaming to be scratched. "Are you almost done? I can't stand sitting still. And my foot is asleep."

"Here's what I have so far." Henry turned the clipboard around so Finley could see.

"I like the way you did my hair," Finley said. "And there's not a freckle out of place!"

"Thanks," said Henry. "I gave you some chocolate chips to help you get ideas, and your pencil and sketchbook in case you get a brainstorm."

Finley laughed. "You thought of everything!"

Henry shook his head. "Something's still missing."

Finley wiggled her toes and made a face. "Yikes! My foot's waking up — it's all tingly and sparkly!"

Henry's eyes lit up. "That's it!" He grabbed some glitter glue and dotted and dripped it across his paper. Then he used his finger to smear it all around. "There," he said. "Olivia's spunk-ified, and you're sparkli-fied!"

"Awesome!" said Finley. "I'm shining!"

Henry held the drawing out to her. "You can keep it if you want."

"Thanks," Finley took it and offered hers to Olivia. "You can keep mine, too. What about yours?"

"Hold on a sec," Olivia said, squinting at her drawing. She added a few final lines, then set it down.

"Wow," said Henry. In the portrait, Henry was sitting under a tree, writing in his notebook. He was wearing his baseball cap and red high-top sneakers. Behind him were softly shaded clouds and smudgy layers of hills.

"I put you under a tree, just like that portrait you liked at the museum," Olivia explained. "You're making one of your lists. And there are some of your books beside you — a bug book and a cookbook."

"The sky is beautiful!" said Finley. "So is the tree — I wish I could climb it right now!"

Finley, Henry, and Olivia put their pictures side by side.

"They look good together!" said Olivia.

"Those are definitely not *bore*-traits," Henry joked.

Finley grinned. "I love making art! I still want to be an artist one day."

"You should," Olivia told her. "You're like an idea factory."

"More like an idea garden," said Henry. "You're always sprouting new thoughts."

"We all are," Finley said. She pointed out the window to the leaf hammocks swaying in the breeze. "Just look what we made together."

Tastes-Like-Fall Pumpkin Bread

Get a grownup to help you make this spicy-sweet fall favorite! Be on the safe side — make sure to have an adult supervise and do the baking!

What You'll Need:

- 3 cups flour
- 2 teaspoons baking soda
- 1 teaspoon salt
- 2 teaspoons cinnamon
- 1 teaspoon nutmeg
- 1 teaspoon cloves
- 1 teaspoon allspice
- 1 (15-ounce) can of pumpkin
- 1 cup oil
- 2 ¼ cups sugar
- 4 large eggs

Note: Cinnamon can be used in place of any of the other spices if you don't have them. You can also add 1–2 cups chopped apples or chocolate chips for some Fin-teresting flavor!

What to Do:

1. Have an adult preheat the oven to 350 degrees.
2. Butter two large loaf pans or four small loaf pans.
3. Mix dry ingredients. Mix wet ingredients in a separate bowl. Mix dry ingredients with wet ingredients.
4. Spoon the batter into prepared pans, filling them about halfway.
5. Bake until the centers of the loaves spring back when pressed, about 40 minutes, depending on the size of your pans. (Have an adult check for you.)
6. Let cool for five minutes, then turn out the loaves onto a wire rack and let cool completely.

Fall Still Life

Make sure to ask an adult to help you find foods to draw!

What You'll Need:

- Foods from your kitchen, preferably fall fruits and veggies like apples, grapes, pears, squashes, pumpkins, and sweet potatoes — but other foods work, too!
- Leaves from outside, for a fall-ish feeling
- A piece of fabric, like a tablecloth, dishtowel, or blanket — or even a piece of clothing like a shirt
- Paper to draw on
- A pencil, and colored pencils, crayons, or markers if you want a splash of color

What to Do:

1. Drape the fabric over a table or chair — make sure to leave some wrinkles!
2. Arrange the foods and leaves on the fabric, with larger items at the back and smaller ones in front.
3. Starting with the objects closest to you, lightly sketch the contours — or outlines — of each

object, paying attention to their general shapes. Once you finish drawing the closest object, move on to the objects next to or behind it.

4. Add some details. Look for the shadows under, on, and between objects and shade them in with the side of your pencil.

5. Add some color if you want, layering your colored pencils, crayons, or markers.

Tip: Don't sit too close while you're sketching — it's easier to get a good perspective from a couple of feet away.

About the Author

Jessica Young grew up in Ontario, Canada. The same things make her happy now as when she was a kid: dancing, painting, music, digging in the dirt, picnics, reading, and writing. Like Finley Flowers, Jessica loves making stuff. When she was little, she wanted to be a tap-dancing flight attendant/veterinarian, but she's changed her mind! Jessica currently lives with her family in Nashville, Tennessee.

About the Illustrator

When Jessica Secheret was young, she had strange friends that were always with her: felt pens, colored pencils, brushes, and paint. After repainting all the walls in her house, her parents decided it was time for her to express her "talent" at an art school — the famous École Boulle in Paris. After several years at various architecture agencies, Jessica decided to give up squares, rulers, and compasses and dedicate her heart and soul to what she'd always loved — putting her own imagination on paper. Today, Jessica spends her time in her Paris studio, drawing for magazines and children's books in France and abroad.